new york debut

carter house girls

new york debut

melody carlson

ZONDERVAN®

ZONDERVAN.com/
AUTHORTRACKER
follow your favorite authors

ZONDERVAN

New York Debut
Copyright © 2009 by Melody Carlson

Requests for information should be addressed to:
Zondervan, *Grand Rapids, Michigan* 49530

Library of Congress Cataloging-in-Publication Data

Carlson, Melody.
    New York debut / by Melody Carlson.
        p. cm. — (Carter House girls ; bk. 6)
        Summary: Life at the Carter house is in an uproar, with Taylor coming home
from rehab treatment, Kriti developing a possible eating disorder, and Eliza creating
competition between the girls for the New York debut at Spring Fashion Week.
        ISBN 978-0-310-71493-4 (softcover)
        [1. Models (Persons) — Fiction. 2. Eating disorders — Fiction. 3. Alcoholism — Fiction.
4. Christian life — Fiction. 5. Interpersonal relations — Fiction. 6. Conduct of
life — Fiction. 7. Boardinghouses — Fiction.] I. Title.
    PZ7.C216637Ne 2009
    [Fic] — dc22   2008040305

Interior design by Christine Orejuela-Winkelman

Printed in the United States of America

09 10 11 12 13 14 15 16 • 22 21 20 19 18 17 16 15 14 13 12 11 10 9 8 7 6 5 4 3 2 1

new york debut

"**WHERE IS OUR TAYLOR?**" asked Grandmother pleasantly. She kept her eyes focused on the road as she navigated her Mercedes through the heavy traffic exiting the air terminal.

DJ hadn't told Grandmother the whole story yet. In fact, she hadn't said much of anything to her this past week, except to leave a brief message explaining that she'd changed her return flight from Vegas, and that she planned to be home two days earlier than expected. Obviously, Grandmother had assumed that Taylor had changed her plans too and was returning with DJ.

"So ... is Taylor on a later flight?" Grandmother persisted.

DJ was tempted to say, "What happens in Vegas stays in Vegas." But she knew Grandmother wouldn't buy that.

"Desiree?" Grandmother glanced at her curiously.

"Taylor is in LA." DJ said the words slowly, wishing she could add something more to her answer, something that would deflect any further questioning ... or blame. But what?

"Visiting her father?"

"No ..."

"Touring with Eva?"

7

"No ..."

"What then?" Grandmother's voice grew slightly irritated as she entered the busy expressway, cutting directly in front of a semi without even using her turn signal. The trucker leaned into his horn, but Grandmother seemed oblivious. "Where is the girl, Desiree? Why isn't Taylor with you? Speak up, please!"

"Taylor is in rehab." DJ sucked in a quick breath, preparing herself for her grandmother's reaction.

"Rehab?" Grandmother turned to stare at DJ with widened eyes. "Whatever for?"

"For alcohol treatment." DJ pointed ahead at the crowded road now. "Watch out!" she cried as the Mercedes wandered over the line and into the center lane.

Grandmother returned her attention to driving, her lips pressed tightly together. Hopefully she was stunned into speechlessness, although DJ knew it wouldn't last long. DJ looked out the window, staring at the stone gray skyline as she twisted the handle of her Gucci bag. Taylor had forced the purse on her right before she went into the rehab facility.

"You keep it," Taylor had told DJ after she'd emptied some personal items into another bag. They were sitting in Taylor's mom's luxurious tour bus that was parked outside of the rehab center. The Gucci bag was on the small dining table, with Taylor and DJ sitting across from each other.

"I can't keep your purse," DJ had told Taylor. "It's way too expensive. Besides, I know how much you love this bag."

"It'll make me feel better to know it's on the outside." Taylor was joking, but DJ could see the tears in her eyes. "For all I know someone in that place might try to steal it from me anyway."

Then they'd just sat there in silence for a few minutes. DJ had worried that this was all a huge mistake ... and that it was all DJ's fault for confronting Taylor in the first place. Not that

DJ didn't want Taylor to get help with her alcohol problem. She most definitely did. But, really, what did they know about this place? And what about the people who ran it? Wouldn't it be better for Taylor to get treatment back in Connecticut? Back where she'd have friends to support her?

"Let's go." Taylor had stood with a determined expression. The driver, who'd been patiently waiting outside for them, now opened the door and smiled uncertainly, asking Taylor if she was ready. She had just nodded solemnly, waiting as he gathered up her designer bags and led the way.

"Are you sure you want to do this?" DJ had asked as they followed him to the main entrance of the facility. But Taylor said nothing. Instead, she'd held her head high, in that haughty Taylor fashion, tossing DJ a narrow-eyed glance. DJ had known immediately what the look meant. It was a warning—keep your mouth shut before I let you have it. And that's just what DJ had done.

Grandmother made a hissing sound through her lips, but continued to drive without speaking. This was a relief since DJ didn't really want to discuss Taylor right now. She was still trying to grasp this strange turn of events herself. It felt surreal. Just a week ago, she'd been so angry at Taylor (and Eliza too). They'd both been totally exasperating in Vegas—drinking, partying, and pretending to be adults, but acting more like spoiled children. Then Eliza left—just as quickly as she'd come. That's when DJ had confronted Taylor, and that's when Taylor had decided to get help. After that, DJ had been mostly on her own, counting the days and hours until she could fly out of there. No matter what others said about the glitz and glamour of Las Vegas, to DJ it would always be lonely and depressing. She was thankful to be back in Connecticut again. Even if it was starting to rain.

DJ had expected to feel relieved after she'd left Taylor at the rehab facility. Really, shouldn't she be thankful that Taylor was finally safe? Instead, DJ felt sad and worried and somewhat responsible. The hardest part was discovering that Taylor wasn't allowed any communication from the outside.

DJ didn't get that. What was the point of cutting Taylor off from everyone? No cell phone calls, email, or anything. It seemed weird — and slightly suspicious. Oh, sure, the rehab place had looked pretty swanky with its beachside location near Malibu. It had manicured grounds, elegant palm trees, and pretty stucco buildings with red tiled roofs. But what if it was some kind of a cult where they brainwashed their patients and promised to fly them off to Jupiter? DJ had seen a movie like that once.

Naturally, DJ was praying for her missing roommate, but she still felt concerned. What if they were mean to Taylor? What if something bad had already happened and Taylor was unable to call for help? What if Taylor never came back? Not only would DJ blame herself, she figured everyone else would too.

DJ jumped to hear Grandmother speaking to her again. "Desiree?" she said sharply. "Are you even listening to me?"

"Sorry . . ." DJ turned to look at her. "What did you say?"

"I was simply inquiring as to whether you girls got into some kind of trouble out there in Las Vegas." Grandmother had exited from the expressway by now, and they were coming into the outskirts of Crescent Cove. DJ was surprised at how thankful she was to see this town — the same town she'd been so eager to escape before Christmas. Not only that, but she missed her friends. She would be happy to see the other Carter House girls again. Well, except for Eliza. DJ wasn't too excited about seeing her. Hopefully Eliza was still in France for a while longer.

"No ..."

"Now I expect you to be completely honest with me, Desiree. Did something happen to precipitate this rather shocking news ... this news that Taylor is being treated for ... for alcoholism?"

"The only thing that happened is that Taylor finally realized that she has a serious drinking problem. Remember, I tried to let you in on this 'shocking news' some time ago."

"Well, yes, I do recall the incident with the vodka bottle. I simply assumed it was a one-time occurrence."

"I told you it wasn't." DJ could hear the edginess in her own voice. But she didn't even care. Really, wasn't this partially her grandmother's fault? Why hadn't she taken DJ's warnings more seriously?

"I do know that girls will be girls, Desiree. You can't have spent as much time in the fashion industry as I have and not know this."

"Were you ever like that?" asked DJ suddenly. "I mean, that 'girls will be girls' bit? Did you do stuff like that? Did you do drugs or alcohol?"

Grandmother cleared her throat. "I certainly wasn't an angel, Desiree, if that's what you're hinting at. However, I did understand the need for manners and decorum. But that was a different era ... people behaved more properly then. Still, over the years, I have witnessed numerous young women whose lives have spun out of control. Beautiful or not, a model won't last long if she is unable to work."

"Isn't that true with everything?"

"Well, yes ... I suppose so."

DJ sighed and looked blankly out the window as Grandmother drove through the small seaside town. She wondered if Conner was back yet. It seemed like years since she'd spoken to him.

"So ... how long is Taylor going to be in ... this rehabilitation facility?"

"I don't know. You should probably call her mom."

"Oh, dear!" Grandmother shook her head as she turned down their street. "That's something else I hadn't considered. I certainly hope that Eva Perez doesn't blame me for her daughter's ... well, for Taylor's drinking problem. Do you think she does?"

"Eva is fully aware that Taylor had this 'drinking problem' long before she came to Carter House."

"Good." Grandmother sighed as she turned into the driveway. "I just hope Taylor's treatment won't prevent her from participating in Fashion Week. That would truly be a disaster."

"Seems like it would be a worse disaster if Taylor didn't get the help she needs."

"Yes, of course, that goes without saying. But I would think that a week or two should be sufficient treatment. Goodness, just how bad can a problem get when you're only seventeen?" Grandmother turned off the engine and looked at DJ curiously.

DJ shrugged, but didn't say anything. The truth was she thought it could get pretty bad, and in Taylor's case it had been scary bad. Plus, it could've gotten much worse. It was mind boggling to think that Taylor had been drinking daily and DJ never even knew it. Oh, she'd known about the binges. But, despite sharing a bedroom, DJ never suspected that Taylor drank every day.

"It's just as well you came home early, Desiree," said Grandmother as they walked into the house. "Already, Casey and Rhiannon are back. And Kriti is supposed to return tomorrow. Eliza will be back on New Year's Eve."

"I'm surprised she didn't want to stay in France for New Year's." DJ hadn't told Grandmother about Eliza's surprise appearance in Vegas. Or the role she had played in helping to derail Taylor.

"As am I. If I were over there, I'd certainly have booked a room in Paris for the big night. Nothing is more spectacular than fireworks over the River Seine. But apparently Eliza has plans with her boyfriend here in town. Imagine—giving up Paris for a teenage boy!"

Of course, DJ knew that Eliza's life of lavish luxury didn't mean all that much to her. Sure she was spoiled, but like a poor little rich girl, Eliza wanted a slice of "normal." Well, normal with a few little extras like good shoes, designer bags, and her pretty white Porsche—not to mention her obsessive need to be first and best at everything. DJ remembered Eliza's confession during their silly Truth or Dare game in Vegas. Although Eliza never would've admitted this if she hadn't been slightly inebriated at the time.

"It's good to be home," DJ proclaimed as her grandmother opened the door. DJ was struggling to drag her baggage up the porch stairs. Naturally, Grandmother didn't offer to help. DJ didn't expect it.

"It's nice to hear you say that, Desiree." Grandmother waited for DJ to come into the house. "And I'm glad to have you back as well." She frowned as she closed the door. "But I'd be disingenuous to say that I'm not severely disappointed that you left Taylor behind. I really didn't expect that from you."

DJ just sighed as she lugged her bags to the foot of the stairs. It figured that Grandmother had decided to blame DJ for Taylor's problems. Why should that even surprise her? Why had she expected anything more?

2

NEW YORK DEBUT

YET WHAT SHE'D SAID WAS TRUE; despite Grandmother's insinuation that it was all DJ's fault that Taylor was in rehab, DJ was glad to be home. Yes, home. For the first time ever, Carter House felt like home. And DJ couldn't wait to see Casey and Rhiannon.

"You're back," yelled Casey from the landing upstairs. Then she dashed down and hugged DJ. "Need some help?"

"Thanks." DJ studied Casey for a moment, trying to figure out what had changed. "Your hair!"

Casey picked up one of DJ's bags, then grinned as she gave her strawberry-blonde hair a shake. "Like it?"

"It's the old you — only better."

"My mom talked me into it — actually she bribed me with a new iPod." Casey patted her short hair. "Besides, the black was getting old. Too melodramatic, don'tcha think?"

"I think you look fantastic, Case! That choppy layered cut makes your eyes look fantastic."

"Your grandmother approved too." Casey grinned. "That doesn't happen too often. At least not with me."

DJ touched her own hair. "Taylor was nagging me to get my highlights redone. But it was so expensive in Vegas, I figured I'd just wait."

Casey lowered her voice as they took DJ's bags up the stairs. "So how'd your grandmother take the news about Taylor?"

DJ stopped at the top of the stairs and stared at Casey. "Did Rhiannon tell you *everything?*"

"Is it supposed to be some big secret?" Casey made a hurt face now. "I wondered why you told Rhiannon and not me. I thought we were friends, DJ."

"I didn't mean to tell anyone, but I sort of spilled the beans with Rhiannon because I was so desperate and didn't know what to do at the time. But then I realized that Taylor might've wanted to keep this all private, you know?"

Casey nodded somberly. "Yeah . . . I do know."

"You should." DJ knew they were both remembering the intervention a few months ago when Casey had stolen DJ's pain pills.

"So, mum's the word?"

"Until Taylor comes back. It's up to her to say something or not." DJ set her bags down by the door to her room, glancing around to be sure no one was around to eavesdrop.

"I can just imagine Eliza's big mouth. It'd be all over the school in no time."

"Speaking of Eliza," DJ said quietly, "that means Kriti too."

"Kriti got here about an hour ago." Casey whispered, nodding toward the room that Kriti and Eliza shared. "The taxi dropped her, and she went straight to her room like something was wrong."

"What do you mean?" DJ whispered back.

"I'm not sure. She just seemed different. Kind of unhappy. I mean, she didn't even speak to anyone."

"Maybe she's just missing her family already."

"Maybe ... but my guess is it's something more."

"I feel sort of guilty about Kriti. I mean, it's like we kind of shoved her at Eliza, like she got stuck with her and can't get unstuck. It's not really fair."

"And Eliza turned her into her yes-girl."

"Anyway, I think we should probably try harder with Kriti. We need to be her friends."

"Eliza might not want to share her."

DJ nodded. Everyone knew how Kriti practically worshiped her heiress roommate and how much Eliza enjoyed it.

"DJ!" Rhiannon came out of her room and threw her arms around DJ. "Welcome home!"

"Man, it is so good to be back. Vegas—for more than a day or two—what a nightmare!"

"At least you got a tan," observed Rhiannon.

"I did get in some pool time," DJ admitted.

Now Rhiannon looked at Casey. "You both look great."

"Thanks to that California sunshine," said Casey.

"Don't make me jealous," said Rhiannon. "It was mostly rain, wind, and cold in Maine."

"But look at you." DJ noticed Rhiannon's outfit. "Is that new?"

"Old and new. My great-aunt gave me some of her old clothes—totally retro, like from the forties and fifties—and I've been altering them." She held out her hands and spun around to make the long circular poodle skirt flair out. "Fun, huh?"

"And cool," said DJ.

"Rhiannon's got all kinds of great stuff," said Casey. "Hats and costume jewelry and scarves and things. I told her she should open a retro shop and get rich."

"Maybe I will someday."

"Or just sell things here in Carter House," suggested DJ. "Between Eliza and Taylor's clothing budget, you could clean up."

"Oh, I almost forgot, DJ, Conner just called," said Rhiannon. "His family just got back from their ski trip, and he said he tried your cell a few times, but it seemed to be turned off."

"More like dead. My flight was early this morning, and I forgot to charge it last night."

"Well, I told him you'd call."

Casey set DJ's bag inside her door. "Speaking of guys, I better check on Garrison—find out if he missed me, or if he got himself another girlfriend while I was gone." She touched her hair. "Think he'll like this?"

"How could he not?" said Rhiannon.

"Later," called Casey as she headed for her room.

"So, how's Taylor?" asked Rhiannon quietly.

DJ pulled Rhiannon into her room and shut the door. "You didn't tell Kriti, did you?"

"No, why would I?"

"I just wanted to be sure. I was surprised that you told Casey."

"Casey told me she'd talked to you while you were in Vegas ... I just assumed she already knew." Rhiannon's green eyes grew wide. "Was I supposed to keep it a secret?"

"I just think we need to respect Taylor's privacy. I told Casey to keep it to herself."

"Absolutely." Rhiannon held up her hand like a pledge. "So, have you talked to her since she went in?"

"They won't let me. I tried to call, and they made it clear that they have a no-communication policy. No email, cell phones ... nothing. It's like a black hole. Kind of freaky."

Rhiannon nodded. "Yeah, it was like that with my mom at first. I think they just wanted to keep her cut off from any bad connections. Then after a while, she earned communication privileges. It's probably the same where Taylor is."

"I hope so." DJ didn't want to admit how much she'd been worrying about this. Not even to Rhiannon.

"I still can't believe Taylor went there willingly."

"Yeah, the wild child . . . putting herself into rehab." DJ shook her head. "Pretty shocking, huh?"

Rhiannon put a hand on DJ's shoulder. "Don't worry about her, DJ. This is a good thing."

"I know." DJ turned away to unzip a suitcase.

"And we're both praying for her."

"Absolutely." DJ pulled her clothes out of her bag and tossed them onto Taylor's neatly made bed. Obviously the work of Inez. "I might as well make myself comfortable in here," she said. "As long as Taylor's gone." Now DJ turned and looked at Rhiannon with worried eyes. "I just hope she's okay."

"I'm sure she's just fine," Rhiannon assured her.

Rhiannon left, and DJ finished unpacking. Then she stood looking at the quiet bedroom, staring at Taylor's side, and suddenly missing her more than ever. DJ told herself this was crazy. Totally nuts. If anything, DJ should enjoy this solitude. Having a room to herself again was a real luxury. And, really, missing Taylor was kind of like missing a toothache.

To distract herself, DJ plugged her cell phone into the charger, then dialed Conner's number. "Heard you called."

"You're back?" His voice sounded happy, and suddenly DJ wished she was with him.

"Yeah, I just flew in this afternoon. It's so good to be home. How about you? When did you get back?"

"Yesterday."

"How was it?"

"Fantastic. Great snow. Nice place. But I did miss you."

"Really?"

"You bet."

"I missed you too."

"Seriously? Wouldn't that be hard to do in Vegas?"

DJ laughed. "Okay, how much did Rhiannon tell you?"

"Just that you were in Vegas. That you'd gone to hang with Taylor." There was a pause now. "Seriously, DJ, what was up with that?"

"I know it sounds pretty random."

"And insane."

"Taylor was lonely. I was bored. Grandmother gave her okay. The next thing I knew I was in Sin City." DJ kind of laughed.

"So . . . how'd it go?"

"We had our ups and downs. But the good news is that I think God was at work. I can't go into all the juicy details . . ."

"Give a guy a break."

"Let's just say that Taylor really talked. Now I understand her a little better."

"Is that even possible?"

"She's been through some really rough stuff."

"Is that why she drags you through rough stuff too?"

"Maybe." DJ was ready for a new subject. "So, what've you been up to, Conner?"

"I just got done shooting hoops, and I'm starving. You want to grab a bite and see a movie or something?"

"I'm probably not good for a late night. I got up around four this morning."

"But that was West Coast time, right?"

"Yeah, but I didn't sleep much before that either."

"Are you awake enough to go to the Hammerhead?"

"Oh yeah."

"See you in a few?"

"I'm already salivating."

"Over me?"

"Actually, I was thinking about the fish and chips."

"Thanks a lot."

But when Conner arrived to pick her up, she threw her arms around him. "I am so glad to see you!"

He hugged her tightly. "Man, I missed you, DJ!"

"Hey, you got a tan too," she pointed out as they walked to his pickup.

"Just my face."

She chuckled. "Well, I did better than that."

"So you girls didn't get into any trouble in Vegas?" he asked as he started the engine.

"Remember what they say . . ."

"What happens in Vegas stays in Vegas?"

She laughed. "That's right."

"Come on," he urged as he drove. "Something must've happened there. I can't imagine two hot babes like you and Taylor strolling around Vegas and not stirring up some kind of trouble. I mean, we are talking about the same Taylor, aren't we?"

"The same, but maybe changing."

"So what happened? Give me the gory details."

"Okay, I'll admit that Taylor did some drinking."

"Big surprise there."

"She gave me a fake ID for Christmas."

"Did you use it?"

"She practically shoved me into the club."

"You went clubbing?"

"Taylor went clubbing . . . I went as her bodyguard."

Conner frowned. "I can't really see you as a bodyguard."

21

"Thanks a lot." She flexed a bicep.

"I know you're strong."

"I can hold my own."

"I just meant, two pretty girls like you and Taylor. You'd *both* need a bodyguard."

"Thanks." She smiled at him. "But I did my best to keep Taylor out of trouble. It was like babysitting. Not much fun."

"I'm still shocked that you went in the first place." Conner parked the truck and helped her out. "You're not really the Vegas type."

"And I will take *that* as a compliment." She linked arms with him as they went into the café. Then, to distract him from more questions about Taylor, she told him about Eva Perez and the concerts and some of the Vegas sights.

"It feels like it's been a year since I saw you." Conner smiled as they sat across from each other. "You look better than ever."

"Back at you."

"I almost got a phone card so I could call you on a pay phone, but I didn't want to get fined."

"Huh?"

"Yeah. Fifty bucks."

"Why?"

"My dad's little game. When we realized our cell phones didn't work at the resort, he challenged us to totally disconnect. To make it interesting, he attached fifty bucks. Anyone caught breaking the rules was fined fifty bucks, but those who didn't were rewarded with a C-note."

"Seriously?"

"Yeah, it was tough at first. We all went through serious withdrawal. But then it was okay." He laughed. "The best part was catching my dad on a pay phone in the ski lodge, and he had to pay me."

"Sounds fun."

"And profitable."

While Conner looked at the menu (which they both probably knew by heart), DJ studied him. His life was so totally different than hers. Sometimes it almost seemed like a dream to hear him talk about it. And sometimes it bugged her to hear him taking his family for granted. Sure, he appreciated them, but he didn't always realize what he had. She mentally compared their Christmases and imagined what it would feel like to spend hers with caring parents and interesting siblings, together at a ski lodge, cut off from the rest of the world and just having good clean fun like that. Meanwhile she'd been in Vegas with Taylor. She sighed.

As much as DJ didn't like feeling jealous of others, particularly her boyfriend, it was hard not to compare her "family" situation to his. Living in a boarding house with a bunch of teenage girls, having someone like Grandmother for her guardian, the whole focus on appearances and modeling ... she wondered how it would feel to switch places with Conner.

Grandmother Dinged Her Fork against her coffee cup, then cleared her throat as if getting ready to make a big speech. It was the morning of New Year's Eve, and everyone except Taylor had returned from Christmas break.

"First of all, I want to welcome you all back to Carter House officially." Grandmother smiled as she turned her attention to Eliza. "I heard you arrived late last night. I do hope your holidays went well."

"Yes. France was very nice. We spent some time on the Riviera and even got in a little skiing at Paradiski."

"Oh, that sounds lovely, dear. I'm surprised you didn't want to stay for the New Year's celebrations."

"I missed my Harry." Eliza smiled in a coy way. "Speaking of Harry ... I know this is very last minute, Mrs. Carter, but he and I wondered if we might have a New Year's Eve shindig here. He had planned to have a small gathering at his parents' beach house, but he just found out it's already promised to friends for the weekend. His parents are having company at his house ... and poor Harry has already invited his guests and arranged for catering, and now he doesn't know what to do."

25

Grandmother frowned slightly . . . or as much as her latest Botox would allow. "I don't know, dear . . . that last party . . . at Halloween . . . got a bit out of hand."

"It did," agreed Eliza. "But that was only because we had party crashers, but that wouldn't be the case this time."

Grandmother placed a finger on her chin as if considering this.

"Naturally, Harry and I would take complete responsibility for everything, from the caterers to the cleaning services afterward," promised Eliza. Then she gave Grandmother her most charming smile. "I told my mother how much you make us all feel at home here, Mrs. Carter. How you treat us as if we're your own family."

DJ suppressed the urge to gag.

"Well . . ." Grandmother sighed loudly. "I suppose a party would be all right. As long as you do as you promise, Eliza. I expect you to take full responsibility for the outcome."

"Absolutely." Eliza nodded.

"I suppose I'll need to cancel my plans with the general. He got us reservations at the country club party, and we were meeting friends."

"Go ahead and go out," urged Eliza. "We'll be just fine. If you like, we could pay Inez or Clara to stick around as chaperones."

DJ couldn't help but roll her eyes at this ludicrous suggestion. Both Clara and Inez knew enough to lie low and keep their mouths shut when it came to some of these little rich girl games. Some chaperones.

"Yes." Grandmother nodded slowly. "I think that would be a good idea."

"Great," said Eliza, folding and placing her napkin off to one side. "I'll have to call Harry and tell him the good news."

"Not quite yet," said Grandmother. "I have some very important and exciting news that I wish to share with everyone first." She cleared her throat for the second time, then launched into a rather long-winded monologue about Dylan's gracious invitation for the Carter House girls to show off his new line during Fashion Week.

"Oh, that is exciting," gushed Eliza.

"We'll all be modeling?" asked Kriti uncertainly.

"Yes, of course. Dylan wants all of you girls to participate." Grandmother looked around the table, pausing at the empty chair where Taylor usually sat. "Including Taylor." Her voice sounded confident, but her eyes clouded ever so slightly. DJ wondered if Grandmother was worried about Taylor too.

"Does this mean we'll have to learn how to walk again?" Casey, as usual, couldn't hide her disinterest. But DJ understood. Already she had suppressed the urge to groan several times this morning. Then, as if reading her thoughts, Grandmother tossed DJ a withering glance. Like she had something to do with Casey's attitude.

"I hope you girls appreciate what a marvelous opportunity this is for all of you." Grandmother looked directly at Casey now. "Spring Fashion Week in New York is one of the fashion events of the season. Everyone who is anyone in the fashion world will be there. You should be thankful for such a privilege."

Casey sighed, but Grandmother continued droning on. "Naturally, we will need to begin practicing at once. I would like to start our classes this upcoming Saturday. And then on every Saturday morning up until the event, which will be the last week of January. I will expect all the girls to meet me on the third floor where we will have a runway in place. I'm having it constructed to the exact proportions of Dylan's catwalk. We'll use it to practice on."

"How long are these practices going to take?" asked DJ.

"We'll begin promptly at nine," said Grandmother. "And we will end at noon with a light lunch."

"Three hours?" DJ couldn't help but grimace.

"We will focus not only on modeling, Desiree, but also manners, grooming, deportment, and other matters that certain young women are in dire need of these days. It's becoming more and more apparent that the younger generation is degenerating by the minute." Grandmother's stern expression suddenly brightened. "In fact, my granddaughter has given me a most delightful idea."

DJ couldn't help herself as a groan escaped. "What now?"

"I shall open these classes to the public. Goodness knows there are dozens of other girls in this town ... girls from good families who are sadly lacking in the social graces. We shall include them." Grandmother clasped her hands together. "For a small fee, of course."

Now DJ groaned even louder.

Grandmother sent her another warning look. "I think you are making the need for such training painfully apparent, Desiree." Grandmother stood with perfect posture and an even expression. "Now, if you will excuse me, ladies, I have some phone calls to make. Have a good day."

"Way to go, DJ," Casey said after Grandmother was out of hearing distance. "Thanks to you, this craziness will be open to the public."

"Are you saying you didn't have something to do with that too?" DJ tossed back.

"Maybe. But now we get to look like fools in front of others."

"You don't think they'll look like fools too?" asked DJ.

"Just a house of fools," added Eliza lightly.

Kriti was the only one not talking. She just sat there looking sad and staring at her untouched slice of whole-grain toast.

"You feeling okay, Kriti?" DJ asked.

"I'm fine." Kriti sat up straighter now.

"Have you been sick?" asked Rhiannon. "You don't seem like yourself."

Kriti nodded. "Actually, I had the flu during the break."

"Too bad," said Rhiannon. "Hopefully, you're over it now."

"Hopefully."

"So when does our beloved Taylor return?" Eliza opened her phone to check for messages.

No one said anything, and Eliza looked up from her phone and focused on DJ. "Don't you know when she's coming back?"

DJ shrugged. "Not really."

"Eliza said that she joined you and Taylor in Las Vegas." This was the most Kriti had said all morning.

"That's right." DJ reached for a second piece of toast.

"So why didn't Taylor come back with you?" Eliza's persistence suggested suspicion.

"I wanted to come home early."

"So is she on her way now?"

"No, not yet." DJ pretended to be absorbed in the spreading of some fake butter on her toast.

"When then?"

"I don't really know." DJ glanced at Rhiannon for help, but Rhiannon was sipping her coffee, and Casey looked totally blank.

"Okay, DJ," said Eliza in a firm tone. "What's up?"

"Nothing is up." DJ just shrugged.

Now Kriti looked interested, or maybe Eliza had kicked her under the table. "I'm curious why you went to Vegas with Taylor."

Eliza laughed. "I'm sure a lot of people are curious."

DJ just shrugged. "To hang with Taylor."

"Please, explain to the class," teased Eliza. "We'd all like to know why Miss Goody-Goody went to Sin City to hang with the devil woman."

"What about you?" countered Casey. "Why did you go, Eliza?"

"For fun."

"First of all, I'm not Miss Goody-Goody." DJ scowled at Eliza. "And Taylor is not the devil woman."

"DJ said she went to keep Taylor company," Rhiannon explained to Kriti. "Taylor was lonely."

Kriti just nodded, but her eyes seemed sad. DJ wondered if Kriti was lonely too.

"DJ went to help keep Taylor out of trouble," added Casey.

"But ..." Eliza's smile turned slightly sinister now. "DJ couldn't do that. Isn't that right, DJ? You couldn't keep our wild child from getting into trouble."

"What about you?" asked DJ.

"What?" Eliza looked innocent.

"You couldn't keep Taylor *or yourself* out of trouble, could you?"

Eliza shook her head. "I didn't get into trouble, DJ. I had a nice little visit and went on my happy way."

DJ pressed her lips together to keep from saying anything more. Why should she play this stupid game?

"So ... tell me." Eliza's eyes narrowed. "Did Taylor get caught at something? Arrested for underage gambling or drinking or—"

"No."

"Come on, DJ. Tell the truth—why didn't Taylor come back with you? That's what she said she was going to do."

"She decided to spend some time in LA before coming back here."

"*Why?*"

"Why not?" DJ looked directly at Eliza.

"She's *not* coming back, is she?" Eliza looked triumphant. "She got into some serious trouble, didn't she? I could tell she was out of control. Like an accident just waiting to happen. What really went down, DJ? Tell us."

"Nothing went down, Eliza."

"But she's not here. And her cell phone is shut down. I know because I already tried to call her. What's up?"

"She's in LA." DJ stood now.

"Why?" Eliza stood and faced her.

"Because she likes the weather down there." DJ was seriously irked now. "Who doesn't?"

"Like it's any of your business," added Casey.

"Like it's not," Eliza shot back at her. Then she smiled sweetly. "But don't worry, I'll get to the bottom of it. Thank you so much for your cooperation." Then she gracefully turned around and walked out of the room like she was the queen of the ball—or maybe queen of the catwalk. DJ suspected that with Taylor's absence, Eliza would attempt to usurp that crown permanently. Not that they were handing out crowns these days. And if memory served, the last crown given wound up on DJ's head!

Still, that was little consolation now. DJ knew that her answer had only temporarily satisfied Miss Nosey. Once school started up and Taylor was still missing, more questions would roll in. DJ would have to come up with better answers. She wished she knew how Taylor wanted these questions answered. Better yet, she wished Taylor would answer them herself!

"It's probably a good thing Taylor's not here," whispered Rhiannon as she, Casey, and DJ went upstairs.

"Why?" Casey asked as they paused by DJ's door.

"This New Year's Eve party."

"Meaning you think it's going to get out of control?" As DJ said this, she knew it was likely.

"Don't you?"

DJ nodded grimly. "And you know what, I don't want to stick around and play cop this time."

"Me neither," admitted Rhiannon.

"I'm with you guys this time." Casey glanced over her shoulder. "But what do we do?"

"Boycott?" suggested Rhiannon.

"How?" DJ asked. "I mean, this is my house too. Do I just let Eliza run me out?"

"You really want to stick around and pick up the pieces?"

DJ considered this. Not only could she get stuck trying to clean up someone else's mess, she might even be blamed if things got out of hand. She was tired of trying to run herd on craziness. "I think you're right. Maybe a boycott is in order."

Rhiannon laughed. "It's not like we've been invited anyway."

"Yeah," said Casey. "This is Harry and Eliza's party, remember?"

"Do you think our rooms will be safe?" Rhiannon addressed this to DJ. "I mean, I've got all those retro clothes I'm working on. I'd hate to see someone go in there while we're gone and mess with my stuff."

Casey nodded. "That's a real possibility if drinking is involved."

"You know," said DJ, "I've thought about asking Grand-mother about getting locks for our doors. I mean, besides those wimpy locks that anyone can pick with a bobby pin."

"Deadbolts," said Casey firmly. "We need deadbolts."

DJ considered this. "I wonder how hard it would be to get something like that installed today."

"I know a locksmith," said Rhiannon suddenly.

"Huh?" Casey frowned. "Why would you know—"

"A friend of my mom's. Mom was always losing keys or locking herself out. It kind of comes with the addiction territory."

"Give him a call," said DJ.

"It's a her."

"Even better." DJ grinned. "Tell her to bill it to Grandmother. I'll explain it later."

"But what are we going to do tonight?" asked Casey. "Where can we go to lie low?"

"Hey, our church usually has some sort of an all-night party on New Year's," said Rhiannon suddenly. "Because I've been out of town, I kind of lost track. Last year it was at the bowling alley."

"All night in a bowling alley?" Casey looked disappointed.

"It could be fun," said DJ. "I haven't bowled in ages."

"We could invite friends," said Rhiannon. "I might ask Bradford."

"I already told Conner I'd do something with him. Maybe he'd like to go."

"As dorky as it sounds ..." Casey made a face. "It could be kind of fun too. I'll call Garrison and see if he's up for it."

"We better check with the church first," said DJ.

"You do that," commanded Rhiannon. "I'll call the locksmith."

"Do we tell Eliza what's up?" asked Casey.

DJ shrugged. "It's not like it's a secret."

"But it's not like we need to report to her," said Casey.

"We probably won't be missed," said Rhiannon.

"But I'd like to make absolutely sure that Grandmother knows where we are," said DJ. And, okay, this was partly just to be responsible since they were supposed to report their whereabouts, but it was also to make it perfectly clear that this was Eliza's party, not theirs. Just in case.

"You're not staying for the party?" asked Grandmother in a disappointed tone.

"We already have plans," said DJ. "I'm sure Eliza won't even miss us."

Grandmother frowned. "Well, it seems a bit rude not to participate. You girls are supposed to be like family to each other, Desiree."

"In that case, isn't it rude for you to go to out with the general to celebrate New Year's, Grandmother? After all, this is your house. You're supposed to be like the parent or guardian here, right?"

Grandmother's brows arched slightly as she pressed her lips together. She was obviously trying to come up with an appropriate answer. "Well, I have arranged for Inez and Clara to be here, Desiree. I see nothing wrong with that."

"And we have arranged not to be here," said DJ lightly. "And we see nothing wrong with that."

Grandmother nodded, and that seemed to end that conversation. DJ grinned and wished her a happy New Year. "See you in the morning," she said as she exited her grandmother's bedroom.

By that afternoon, their plans were secured. DJ put their names on the list for the church's all-night party, which would be at the bowling alley again. Rhiannon's locksmith friend came and put deadbolts on their doors. By five thirty, amidst the chaos of caterers and party preparations, the three girls slipped out the back door and hopped into DJ's car—destination: diner.

"Bradford invited us to stop by his mom's gallery before the bowling alley," said Rhiannon as they entered the restaurant.

DJ laughed as they sat down at a table. "That's kind of bizarre, isn't it? First we go and experience a bit of culture in an art gallery, then end up at the greasy bowling alley."

"It's diverse anyway."

"Hey, that looks like Haley and her friends," said Casey in a slightly hushed tone.

DJ looked up in time to see Haley, Amy, and Bethany coming into the diner. DJ hadn't seen Haley since she'd visited her in the hospital in November—after Haley had tried to end her life with an aspirin overdose. Everyone at school had pretty much heard about it, and most of them assumed it was because of Conner breaking up with her. And it was no secret that Haley's parents had sent Haley to some kind of treatment center for help.

"I heard she was supposed to be back in school after the New Year," said Rhiannon.

"Do you want to go someplace else, DJ?" asked Casey. "I mean, is this going to be weird?"

"No, of course not. I told you guys that Haley and I are okay now." To prove it, DJ called out to Haley.

"Hey, DJ," said Haley with a smile. "How's it going?"

DJ hurried toward Haley now and actually hugged her. "Great. And it's really good to see you. How are you?"

"I'm okay. I've been home a couple of weeks now."

"You look good," said DJ nervously. "And it really is great to see you." Okay, DJ knew she was repeating herself now. But she didn't know what to say. She hadn't really expected to see Haley tonight. "I've been praying for you."

"Thanks." Haley sighed. "I can use all the help I can get."

As usual, Haley's protective friends were studying DJ closely, almost as if they still blamed DJ for all of Haley's troubles. To be honest, DJ still sometimes blamed herself. But she knew that wasn't the real reason behind Haley's problem. "Are you guys doing anything special for New Year's?" asked DJ as they all waited for the hostess.

Haley just shook her head.

"There's an all-night party at the bowling alley," said DJ suddenly. "It's hosted by the church, but they told me today that any local teens are welcome. We're going."

"At the bowling alley?" Haley looked dubious.

"Yeah, pretty corny," said Casey. "But we're going to make the best of it."

"You should come too," urged Rhiannon.

"Yeah," agreed DJ, glancing at Amy and Bethany. "All of you."

"Well, we'll think about it," said Haley as the hostess motioned for them to follow her.

"The doors get locked at nine o'clock sharp," warned DJ.

"Do you think they'll come?" asked Casey.

"I hope so," said DJ. "I think it would be good for Haley to be around her friends again."

"What about Conner?" asked Casey. "Will Haley get jealous if she sees you two together?"

"No." DJ shook her head. "Haley assured me when she was in the hospital that she was over that."

"But what if that was then ..."

"I'm not concerned." DJ forced a smile.

"Well, I'm praying that she comes," said Rhiannon as the waitress came to take their order. DJ decided she'd be praying the same thing. The truth was, it did worry her a little. It would be the first time that Haley had been around them — with DJ and Conner together. Still, that might be good for Haley to see. Maybe it would help her to deal with it and keep moving on. At least DJ hoped that would be the case.

4

NEW YORK DEBUT

AS IT TURNED OUT, Haley and her friends did come to the all-night party—and everything went fine. To DJ's surprise, it was actually fun and not simply an easy escape from Eliza and Harry's party. Of course, there were moments when DJ wondered what might be going on at Carter House. Chances are it would be a quiet party where alcohol was served and no one got too crazy or out of control. DJ supposed it was possible. Even so, she was glad not to be part of it. She was equally glad that Taylor wasn't around to be part of it either. That alone might keep things calmer.

Still, as she drove Casey and Rhiannon back home the next morning, she was thankful they'd had the forethought to get locks on their doors. At least they could be assured that their rooms would still be intact.

"Hey, look, Harry's Jeep is still here," pointed out Rhiannon.

"A couple of other cars too," noticed Casey.

"Don't tell me they let the guys spend the night." DJ groaned and pulled into the driveway, blocking the car that belonged to Seth Keller, Taylor's most recent boyfriend. DJ wasn't terribly surprised that Seth had come even though Taylor wasn't there. For all DJ knew, he might even have a new girlfriend by now. He was like that.

But when they got inside, the house was surprisingly quiet. And trashed—totally and thoroughly trashed.

"Hello?" called DJ, suddenly feeling very uneasy. What on earth had gone on here? And where was everyone?

"Maybe we should go back outside," said Casey quietly.

"Why?" asked Rhiannon as she cautiously approached the stairway.

"Because it looks like a crime scene," whispered Casey.

"It *is* a crime scene!" Inez popped out of the dining room wearing yellow rubber gloves and a very grim expression.

"What happened?" asked DJ with wide eyes.

Inez scowled. "Crazy kids … alcohol … madness …" Then she resorted to Spanish, ranting in a way that suggested she was more than just a little fed up with adolescents.

"That's too bad," said DJ. "Do you want us to help clean up?"

"No!" Inez held up her hands. "Miss Eliza is going to clean up."

"You mean she hired a cleaning service."

"No. Your grandmother says that Miss Eliza will clean this up herself. No help. No cleaning service. Miss Eliza will be paying her debt to society."

DJ wasn't so sure. "But how can Grandmother force Eliza to do this?"

"Don't worry. Your grandmother has it all worked out with the police."

"The police?"

"Yes. They came here late last night. They took most of the kids with them."

40

"Who called the police?"

Inez got a sly look. "I'm not saying."

DJ smiled grimly. "I don't blame anyone for calling the police."

"Your grandmother had to go and get Eliza and Kriti out of the slammer. Lucky for Kriti, she was not drinking. Eliza was charged as a minor."

"Do her parents know?"

"Mrs. Carter is dealing with it." Inez lowered her voice. "Clara and I will supervise Miss Eliza to make sure she does all the work. She's in the kitchen now." Inez smiled wickedly. "She is learning to scrub floors. Toilets are next."

Imagining a hung-over Eliza cleaning a toilet, DJ couldn't help but giggle. Soon all three of them were giggling, covering their mouths as they raced up the stairs to avoid being heard, then laughing so hard that there were tears streaking down their faces.

"I am so glad we didn't stick around here," said Casey as she wiped her cheeks. "I almost changed my mind at the last minute when Garrison started making fun of the whole bowling thing."

"So, do you think Harry and Seth got arrested?" asked Rhiannon.

"That's my guess," said DJ. "Since their cars are still here."

Now Kriti emerged from the room she and Eliza shared. She nodded glumly, as if she'd been listening. "It was a mess."

"But you weren't drinking?" DJ studied Kriti, noticing that there were dark circles beneath her eyes. Probably from lack of sleep.

"No, I told Eliza that after getting so sick at the ski weekend, I had given up alcohol altogether."

"Good for you."

"But I still had to go to the police station." Kriti had tears in her eyes now. "It was so scary. My parents would be so angry if they knew."

"They don't know?"

"Not yet. They are on a business trip."

"Oh ..." DJ nodded. "But you weren't charged with anything, Kriti. You shouldn't get into trouble."

"Where were you guys?" asked Kriti sadly.

They explained, and Kriti just nodded.

"Maybe we should've invited you too," said Rhiannon. "I'm sorry."

Kriti just shook her head. "I wouldn't have gone."

"Why not?" demanded DJ. "Was it better to get in trouble?"

"No, but it's better not to get Eliza mad. She's my only friend."

"We're your friends too," insisted DJ.

But Kriti didn't look convinced. "I'm tired," she said. "Please, excuse me."

"Poor Kriti," Rhiannon said quietly after the door closed.

"It's like she's Eliza's puppet," said DJ.

"Or slave."

"Well, maybe we should emancipate her," suggested DJ.

"It won't work unless she wants it." Rhiannon sadly shook her head.

The girls got out their keys now, letting themselves into their rooms to catch up on some much-needed rest. But, once inside her room, DJ couldn't help but notice how it seemed strangely quiet ... as if something ... rather someone was missing. She had just emerged from the shower and was about to hop into bed for a long winter nap when she heard someone loudly knocking on her door. She hurried over to unlock it, desperately hoping that it was Taylor.

"Grandmother?"

"I wish to speak to you, Desiree."

"Here?"

"Here is fine." Grandmother stepped into the room, then before closing the door, she paused to examine the deadbolt.

"First of all, when did you get that lock put on your door?"

"Yesterday."

"Why?"

"Because I knew that Eliza's party might get out of control, and I didn't want my room trashed. As it turned out, I'm glad that I got it in time. Rhiannon and Casey got one too. You'll receive a bill next week."

Grandmother sighed and sadly shook her head as she sat down in the window seat. She looked very tired and much older than usual. "I don't know what to do, Desiree."

"What do you mean?"

She held up her hands in a hopeless gesture. "Everything is falling apart."

DJ frowned. "You mean because you let Eliza have her stupid party and she brought in alcohol?"

"Yes . . . yes. Then there's this business with Taylor. I'm afraid I'll have to cancel Fashion Week with Dylan. I just don't know what to do."

Okay, the truth was that nothing else would make DJ happier. But, at the same time, she knew how much her grandmother had wanted this. She also knew that Rhiannon was looking forward to seeing the fashion industry up close.

"I don't see why you need to cancel everything, Grandmother."

Grandmother looked up with a surprised expression. "How can I not cancel everything? The truth is, I'm afraid I will have to shut down Carter House altogether. I will have to send all the girls home."

"Even me?" Now DJ was slightly worried. The last thing she wanted was to end up back with her dad, the twins, and her stepmom. Nothing could be worse. Suddenly, the stakes were rising.

"I don't know what else to do, Desiree. I'm afraid I'm just too old for this sort of thing. I thought I could handle it at first, but now I'm not sure. The general even questioned my sensibilities last night when I was called to the police station."

"I'm sure that was hard."

"And humiliating." Grandmother was actually wringing her hands now. "The sergeant at the station even suggested that I was in over my head. Actually those were his exact words. Oh, dear ... I feel like such a failure."

"Well, you are partly to blame, Grandmother. You allowed Eliza to have that party."

"Yes ... but she promised—"

"Eliza is a teenager," pointed out DJ. "She doesn't always tell the truth."

"But I trusted her."

"I don't see why."

Grandmother looked up and studied DJ now. "Did you and the other girls know what was going on here?"

"We had our suspicions. And I've tried to tell you about this before, Grandmother. But, you have to admit that Eliza and Taylor have been your favorites and—"

"I don't have favorites."

"Yes, you do. We all know it. Eliza and Taylor have the most model potential, and, because of that, you seem to turn your head to their problems. Right from the very start, both those girls brought alcohol into the picture. I tried to warn you, and you gave me your 'girls will be girls' spiel."

"Well, it seems you were right, Desiree. It seems I have failed."

"Meaning you're going to quit?" DJ stood up now. "I never thought of you as a quitter, Grandmother. That surprises me."

"I am not a quitter." Grandmother used a lace-trimmed handkerchief to daub at her eyes, although DJ wasn't sure if she was actually crying or just being dramatic.

"But you're going to give up just because Eliza did something stupid?"

"I was stupid to trust the girl."

DJ pointed her finger in the air. "Exactly!"

"So, I suppose you are saying I shouldn't trust any of you . . . about anything . . . ever?"

"Something like that. I mean, you don't need to be like the Gestapo, but you should realize that we are still teenagers and we need some supervision."

"But you, Rhiannon, and Casey . . . you girls made the choice not to be here last night."

"That's right."

Grandmother brightened now. "That shows that at least three of my girls have some sense."

"Just not your favorite three."

"As I said, I do not have favorites."

DJ shrugged.

"And there is hope for Taylor. After all, she is getting help," said Grandmother with fresh optimism.

"Yes. And if it's any consolation, Kriti is not like Eliza. She doesn't like to drink or party. It's just that Eliza seems to have Kriti under her thumb."

Grandmother pressed her lips together, as if in deep thought.

"Another thing, Grandmother. Kriti seems to be very unhappy. In fact, I'm a little worried about her."

Grandmother seemed to consider this.

"I don't think that Eliza is a good influence on her and—"

"I know just the answer!"

"What?"

"Kriti will move in with you."

"Me?" Suddenly DJ wasn't so sure.

"With Taylor gone, Kriti can share—"

"But Taylor will be coming back and—"

"If Taylor desires to room with you, that's fine. But we don't know for sure when Taylor is returning. In the meantime, Kriti shall be your new roommate, Desiree. It's settled."

Okay, DJ knew that she shouldn't be so selfish. But she did not want to share a room with Kriti. The truth was, she would rather have Taylor, wildness and all, for a roommate. And DJ knew that was wrong. Plus it made no sense. Why would DJ rather have Taylor with all her problems? Maybe because, on some levels, she could relate to her. But DJ didn't really get Kriti. For one thing, she was so studious and quiet. It's like she was a shadow. Or like Rhiannon said, a puppet. She always seemed so needy. Like she had to have someone to lead her around and tell her what to do, how to act, what to think. DJ wasn't sure she wanted that someone to be her.

"No arguments, please," insisted Grandmother as she reached for the door. "I will inform Kriti immediately. She can transfer her things while Eliza is performing her cleaning duties. You may take Taylor's things over to Eliza's room."

DJ couldn't tell if Kriti was unhappy with the room change or just unhappy in general. She said very little as they transferred Taylor's things for hers. This was a challenge in itself since Eliza had already hogged most of the closet space, and now DJ was forced to divide it equally, which meant that Eliza would soon discover a heap of her own clothes, bags, and shoes on her bed. Probably about ten thousand dollars' worth of merchandise, maybe more. Of course, DJ had no doubts that Eliza would take full advantage of Taylor's side of the room until Taylor returned. What would happen then was anyone's guess.

As soon as the room switch was complete, Kriti set up her laptop on the small desk and went straight to work. Funny, but it had never occurred to either Taylor or DJ to use the desk as a desk. For one thing, Taylor rarely did homework. And when DJ did hers, she usually opted for her bed or the window seat. Now it seemed odd to see the desk actually in use. Naturally DJ didn't mention this.

Dinner was a somber affair that evening. Eliza was obviously in a snit, but unable to make a fuss since she knew she was still in the doghouse. Kriti seemed to be pouting as well and, consequently, barely seemed to touch her food. But it was Grandmother who made everyone uncomfortable. Not only was she stern and in lecture mode, but she was obsessed with perfect manners. It was as if she thought she could make up for, or perhaps undo, the past five months in one meal. And it figured that as dinner came to an end, it seemed Grandmother's patience was doing likewise.

"Sit up straight, Casey!" she said for the third time. "Butter knife, Rhiannon!" She sounded like Sergeant Etiquette as she barked out her brisk commands. "Chew with your mouth shut, DJ. Kriti, at least pretend that you are enjoying your meal." Eliza was the only one who escaped Grandmother's manners radar, and DJ suspected this was only because Eliza, trained by the best, knew how to act perfect ... when perfection was required.

"May I please be excused, Grandmother?" DJ inquired as politely as possible. The tension in the room was making her stomach hurt.

"Not until I remind everyone that we will be having our Saturday modeling session tomorrow. We will begin promptly at nine." She cleared her throat. "I feel it's only fair to warn you girls, I have come precariously close to canceling Fashion Week altogether. In fact, I am still not convinced that we will be participating."

Eliza's jaw tightened, and Rhiannon's disappointment showed in her eyes as Grandmother continued. "However, I have decided that it will do us no harm to be prepared just in case we do participate in Fashion Week. I have decided not to inform poor Dylan otherwise, just yet anyway. In the case that I am disappointed in any of the Carter House girls, I will consider replacing them with some of the other young women who will be in attendance in our sessions. I hope you understand the significance of this." She turned to DJ. "Yes, Desiree, you may be excused."

"Thank you." DJ stood and left. She wished she could leave the house too, but thanks to Eliza's stupidity last night, all the girls were on some kind of house arrest for the next few days. No one was to go out, and no one was to come visit — period. Grandmother had made that crystal clear as soon as they'd sat down to eat. And, although it was unfair, DJ couldn't help but think it was about time Grandmother put her foot down. She just hoped that she'd have the good sense to realize that her new disciplinary tactics might need to be adjusted and administered on a person-by-person basis.

The house was slowly coming back together, but Eliza's work was far from done yet. Despite her attempt to pressure Kriti into helping this afternoon, DJ had stood up to her. "No, Kriti cannot help you," she'd said firmly. "This is your punishment, not hers." Then later, according to Casey and Rhiannon, Eliza had even resorted to bribery. Naturally, they resisted, although Rhiannon said the rather large cash offer was tempting. But Casey told Eliza where she could put her money.

Later that evening, DJ learned through Conner that Harry and Seth were getting off pretty lightly since this was their first offense — or rather the first time they'd been caught.

"It sounds like they'll do some public service and take a mandatory class about the dangers of underage drinking," he told her on the phone.

"Too bad they don't have to come over here and help Eliza clean up this mess." Then she reconsidered. "Although that might turn into fun and games, and it's supposed to be punitive." Then she told him how she'd accidentally walked into the powder room downstairs, finding Eliza down on her knees, with Inez supervising, as she scrubbed what looked like a vomit-encrusted toilet.

"Oh, man." He chuckled. "I'd like to see that for myself."

"The queen ruling her throne." DJ laughed, then felt slightly guilty. "I guess I'm not being very nice."

"Eliza is getting what she deserves."

"Unfortunately, so are we." DJ sighed. "Eliza's detention is being applied to the whole household for the time being."

"That seems a little harsh."

"Yeah, but in a way I'm glad. At least Grandmother is taking this whole thing seriously. It's about time."

"I hope Harry and Seth's parents are taking it seriously."

"Wouldn't it be better if Harry and Seth took it seriously themselves?"

"Or at least think twice before they do this again."

"I hope so. I don't see why so many kids our age think that getting wasted is fun. Especially when it hurts others." Of course, she wasn't only thinking about the New Year's partiers now. She wondered how Taylor was doing. It had been a week without hearing a single word from her. What was going on? What was she thinking? Was she okay? And was she ever coming back?

5

NEW YORK DEBUT

ONCE SCHOOL STARTED UP AGAIN, Grandmother lifted the house arrest on everyone except Eliza and Kriti. "I expect both you girls to come home directly after school," she told them at breakfast. Neither girl argued. Kriti probably didn't care. In fact, it seemed like she didn't care about much these days. DJ thought maybe she was depressed, but she didn't know why. Eliza, on the other hand, looked ticked. Beneath that smooth veneer of no emotion, DJ could tell that Eliza was seething. Yet she didn't say anything. DJ suspected that Grandmother was threatening to call her parents if Eliza refused to toe the line. Whatever the case, maybe it would prove a good wake-up call for Eliza.

"Aren't you riding with me, Kriti?" asked Eliza as the girls were heading out of the house.

"Oh, yeah." Kriti nodded and slowly trudged behind Eliza out to the car.

"What's wrong with Kriti?" asked Rhiannon as she got into the backseat of DJ's car.

"Yeah," said Casey as she climbed in front. "She's like the walking dead. What's up with her, DJ?"

51

"I have no idea."

"Does she talk to you?"

"Hardly. I ask her a question, and she gives me the briefest possible answer. She studies a lot."

"Do you think something happened to her during Christmas break?"

"Maybe something with a guy?" suggested Casey.

"I thought she and Josh Trundle were kind of an item," said Rhiannon.

"I asked her about him," admitted DJ, "and it sounded like there might still be something there. Although she wasn't very enthusiastic."

"She's not enthusiastic about anything," said Casey.

"And we know it's not because of having her room switched," Rhiannon pointed out. "Because she was already acting different before that."

"Well, I'm going to try to figure it out," DJ declared. "I've been praying for her. I've realized that I haven't been much of a friend to her."

"None of us have," admitted Rhiannon.

"Yeah, we kind of just let Eliza take her over." DJ stopped for the traffic light. "It's like we handed Kriti over and never thought twice about it."

"It's not like Kriti minded."

"Or she was too polite to show it."

"We were too busy to notice," said DJ.

"Well, let's all pray for her today," said Rhiannon.

"Absolutely," agreed DJ.

But Casey just shrugged like she was unsure.

"Don't you *ever* pray?" asked Rhiannon.

"I don't know ..." Casey's voice was quiet now.

"I thought you were returning to your faith," said Rhiannon. "You said that things were changing."

DJ didn't know what to say as she pulled into the school parking lot. She knew this was still a touchy subject for Casey. As much as Rhiannon seemed to assume that Casey had "turned a corner," DJ had never been completely convinced.

"I'm thinking about it," said Casey. "But I'm still not totally sure. And, most of all, I don't want to be a hypocrite."

"Meaning you think we are?" asked Rhiannon.

They were all getting out of the car now, and Rhiannon was looking curiously at Casey, expecting an answer.

"No . . . that's not it," said Casey. "You guys seem pretty sincere about it. If anything, it's you and DJ that got me thinking about God again, which is pretty surprising considering that I gave it all up a few years ago." She laughed. "Trust me, the last thing I expected was to come out to Connecticut and have some kind of faith experience. If anything, I came out here thinking that I was going to . . . well, raise hell."

DJ snickered. "I think that's what Grandmother thought when she first saw you too."

"But you've changed," persisted Rhiannon. "And not just on the outside either, Casey."

"Maybe . . ." Casey shrugged. "But some things take time."

"I know what you mean." DJ nodded as she adjusted her bag over her shoulder. "It took time with me too."

"You're absolutely right," agreed Rhiannon. "Sorry if I sound too pushy. I guess I just want us all to be on the same page."

"I think we are." Casey sounded slightly defensive now. "I mean, for the most part."

"We are," said DJ. "Being open is really all we can ask, right, Rhiannon?"

Rhiannon nodded, but DJ suspected she was disappointed. Maybe it was because her own faith was so vital to her that she wanted everyone to have the same thing. And DJ totally got that. She wanted everyone to make a commitment to God too. But she also understood where Casey was coming from. She knew that Casey, like DJ, would have to find her faith on her own terms. Or maybe on God's own terms. Rhiannon could talk all she wanted, but Casey would have to get to that place on her own. But at least she seemed to be listening.

"I can't promise to pray ... but how about if I send good thoughts in Kriti's direction," offered Casey. "Will that work?"

"I think it's a great start," said DJ.

"Yeah, just try to send them via God, okay?"

Casey laughed. "Fine, Rhiannon. I'll try to send them via God."

DJ's first class this semester was an advanced PE course called Personal Training. Of course, both Taylor and Eliza had teased her for this choice when she'd mentioned it last semester. Not that DJ cared what they thought. Mostly she wanted to make sure she stayed in shape for spring soccer. Swimming had helped a lot, but when the season ended, she was still ready for more.

"Looking good, DJ," said Ms. Jones as DJ completed her weight repetitions.

"Thanks." DJ smiled. "It feels good to get a solid workout after Christmas break."

"How's your leg feeling?"

"Just fine. It doesn't hurt at all."

"Really?" Ms. Jones smiled. "Because Coach Henderson was asking about you."

"About me?" DJ knew that Henderson had just started coaching girls' basketball this year.

"Yeah. It seems the girls had a pretty slow start to basketball season, and he was asking me about some of my volleyball girls."

DJ nodded. "Oh, yeah, Casey is pretty good at hoops. Have you talked to her?"

"No. But I told the coach I'd talk to you. What do you think? Are you strong enough to play yet?"

DJ considered this. "I'd probably have to check with my doctor, but I'm sure there's a possibility."

"Well, if you're interested, I'm pretty sure that Coach Henderson would like to discuss this with you."

"Even though I missed the first few weeks?"

"You were on swim team, DJ. Remember, we make exceptions when the athlete is involved in another sport. Plus there was your leg."

DJ brightened. "It'd be fun to do basketball . . . and it would keep me in shape for soccer."

"If it works, I know the team would love to have you."

"Do you think Coach Henderson would let Casey play too?"

"I don't know why not."

So by the end of the day, DJ had not only put in a call to her doctor, but she'd also talked to the coach, and he agreed to let Casey come out with DJ. "Just get me your doctor's okay first," he said. "We don't want you reinjuring that leg."

"I'm on it," said DJ. "I'll get back to you."

He grinned. "And don't say I said this, but we could really use some skill on that team."

She laughed. "I can't make any promises, but I do like to play."

After school, she turned on her phone to discover a message from the receptionist at the doctor's office, saying that the doctor had already signed DJ off for sports participation at her final appointment, so she was good to go. "Just don't go too hard," she warned. "The doctor says to use common sense."

"Good news," DJ told Casey as they met in the locker bay. "I'm going out for basketball."

"Huh?"

"And you are too."

"What are you talking about?"

So DJ filled her in. "Come on, Casey, it'll be fun. The season's half over, so it's not like a huge commitment."

Casey considered this. "It does sound kind of fun. And it's a good way to keep the weight down. I swear I put on ten pounds during the holidays. It's like there was food everywhere, and I just kept eating."

"So are you in?"

"I'm in."

Just then, DJ spotted Rhiannon and Bradford walking toward them. "Hey," called DJ as she waved them over.

Rhiannon smiled. "What's up?"

DJ explained about basketball and asked if Rhiannon could find another way home. "Maybe you could catch a ride with Eliza and Kriti."

"I can take her home," offered Bradford. And that worked for Rhiannon, so DJ and Casey were free to head on down to the girls' gym, where they dressed down and joined the team. Unlike volleyball season, this time their reception from the team was pretty warm. So much had changed since then.

"As you know," announced the coach, "we do allow players to try out for the team in midseason if they've been participating in another sport in the previous season. DJ was on swim team, and Casey was in volleyball."

"So this is a tryout?" asked Casey.

He nodded. "Yeah. But we'll just do practice as usual. If you girls don't cut the mustard, we'll have to let you go."

Suddenly DJ felt pressure. But it was the kind of pressure she liked. Unlike practicing the catwalk and being teased by girls like Eliza, this was something that DJ was naturally good at. It took only a few times up and down the court before she felt herself falling into the rhythm of the scrimmage. She knew to take it easy and not put too much stress on her leg, but she also knew that she was playing well. So was Casey. By the end of practice, the other players were giving high fives and welcoming them to the team.

"Our next game is Wednesday," said the coach as the girls headed back to the locker room.

"Sounds good," said DJ.

"Thanks, Coach," added Casey.

"Hey, you two," called out Haley as Casey and DJ went into the locker room. "What are you doing here after school?"

"Basketball," said DJ. "You must be doing gymnastics."

Haley glanced around the crowded, noisy locker room as if she felt self-conscious, then lowered her voice. "I missed the beginning of the season ... you know ... but Coach Provost said it was okay to come out anyway."

"How's it going?" asked DJ.

"It feels good to be working out again."

"That's great," said DJ. "Is it hard to catch up?"

Haley shrugged. "Not really. I'd been practicing while I was, well, you know ..." She glanced around nervously. "Elsewhere."

"Good for you," said DJ.

"Yeah. And therapeutic too." Haley smiled now. "And guess what?"

"What?" DJ waited.

"I'm going to come to your grandmother's model training sessions too."

"Cool," said DJ.

"I think it'll be fun." Now she got a funny expression, and DJ wasn't sure what it meant. "Guess what else?"

"What?"

"Madison Dormont and Tina Clark and some of their friends are coming too."

DJ cringed.

But Casey actually cussed. "That means I have to spend every Saturday morning with stupid Madison and Tina!" She turned to DJ. "How is this fair?"

DJ just shrugged. "Life's not fair."

Haley's mouth twisted into a half smile. "Anyway, I thought you guys might appreciate a little heads-up."

"Thanks ... I guess." DJ just shook her head. None of the Carter House girls would be too happy to hear that Madison and Tina were going to be spending Saturdays with them. Not only had they gotten off to a bad start with these girls last fall, but DJ had probably earned the number-one spot on Madison's hate list during the last fashion show. They had both wanted to wear the same dress, but DJ had gotten it first. Then when Madison snatched it, Taylor had stepped in to help, and things had gotten ugly. Of course, DJ hadn't made any more points with Madison when she'd won the title of homecoming queen shortly after that. In fact, DJ was pretty sure that Madison hated her.

"I just don't understand why Madison and Tina actually want to take Grandmother's classes," muttered DJ as she and Casey got dressed. "I mean, of their own volition. I so do not get this."

"Me neither." Casey shook her head. "And it's not like anyone is forcing them to do it either."

"Well, it's not going to make Saturday mornings any more pleasant for any of us." DJ zipped her jeans and sighed.

"Maybe Madison will do something stupid again—like the stunt she pulled at the Founders Day fashion show. Maybe she'll get your grandmother riled up and get herself kicked out of the sessions." Casey snickered. "Hey, maybe we could help her."

"No," said DJ. "That would be wrong, Casey."

"I don't see why. Everyone knows Madison and Tina are the enemy."

"And we're supposed to love our enemies."

"Maybe you are … but I haven't exactly signed up for all that yet."

"Yet."

Casey smirked at her. "Yeah, right … I'm working on it."

After dinner that night, DJ went to her room to do some homework. She expected to find Kriti doing the same, but to DJ's surprise, Kriti was down on the floor by her bed doing abdominal crunches. However, she jumped to her feet as soon as DJ came into the room. She looked uneasy, and her face was flushed, but whether it was from the exercise or embarrassment, DJ wasn't sure.

"I didn't mean to interrupt you," said DJ quickly. "Don't let me stop you from working out."

Kriti hesitated. "Well, okay."

"I mean, if anyone is into physical fitness, it's me."

So Kriti returned to her position on the floor, doing crunch after crunch.

"I think exercise is as good for the inside of a person as it is for the outside," continued DJ as she opened up her geometry book. And, because she didn't want to make Kriti uncomfortable, she pretended to ignore her. But she couldn't ignore the fact that Kriti was doing like a hundred abdominal crunches. Or so it seemed. It wasn't like DJ was counting. But finally she knew she couldn't keep her mouth shut. "Wow, Kriti." She set her math book aside. "That's really a lot of crunches. Why so many?"

Kriti paused on her back, answering breathlessly. "Eliza said it helps."

"Helps what?"

"You know …"

"No, to be honest, I don't know. I mean, like I said, I'm into fitness. But I like a balanced workout, you know? What did Eliza say it helps to do?"

Kriti sat up now. "You know … to trim your tummy and to lose weight."

DJ blinked. "But you don't need to lose weight, Kriti."

Kriti firmly shook her head as she stood and patted her midsection. "You are wrong."

"What do you mean I'm wrong?" DJ frowned. "How much can you possibly weigh? I'll bet that you're barely over a hundred pounds soaking wet."

"You're wrong about that too."

"So. You look great, Kriti."

"No. Eliza said I'm too heavy for my height."

"What does Eliza know?"

"She knows that I'm fat."

"*Fat?*" shrieked DJ. "You are *not* fat, Kriti."

"You're just being nice."

"I am not nice. And the truth is you are not fat, Kriti."

"Yes, I am. And during the holidays I put on a pound."

"A pound?" DJ laughed. "Well, you should be proud. I think I might've put on five. Casey thinks she put on ten."

"You're exaggerating."

"No, I'm not exaggerating. Even though I don't weigh myself, I'm sure I could've put on some weight."

"You don't weigh yourself?"

"No. Why should I?"

Kriti looked confused.

"I mean, who cares what you weigh … as long as you're healthy?"

"Eliza cares."

"Well, she's neurotic."

Kriti didn't look convinced.

"Well, I don't care," declared DJ. "Really, I'm not worried about it."

"Why not?"

"Why should I be?"

"Because of modeling."

DJ rolled her eyes. "So?"

Kriti shrugged. "Well, in your case, it doesn't matter. You and the others are so tall, you don't look short and fat like I do."

"You do *not* look short and fat, Kriti."

"At least Eliza was honest with me."

"Eliza is nuts."

"No. She's been helping me."

"Helping you to do what?"

"To get in shape. To lose weight."

"Oh, Kriti." DJ groaned. "You're taking this modeling stuff way too seriously."

"If you were me, you'd take it seriously too."

DJ felt like she was banging her head against a brick wall now. It was like Eliza had poisoned Kriti. Or brainwashed her. DJ just hoped it hadn't gone too far. Kriti continued to do what seemed a pretty extreme exercise routine. She moved out into the hall, where DJ peeked to discover that Kriti was going up and down the stairs. Quietly, so that she wouldn't disturb anyone.

"How many times do you do that?" asked DJ as Kriti came down from the third floor for about the tenth time.

"It depends."

"On what?"

Kriti shrugged, then continued on down to the first floor. But DJ followed her. "What does it depend on, Kriti?"

Kriti turned around and headed up again. "On what I eat."

"Meaning?"

But Kriti didn't answer. And she didn't stop on the second floor, but kept going up. DJ returned to her room and shook her head. DJ wondered if it was time for another intervention. A different kind of intervention perhaps, but something needed to be done to help Kriti see that there was a problem here. Although DJ had no idea how to go about it. Kriti seemed stubbornly set in her opinions. Thanks to Eliza!

One thing DJ knew for sure, she was going to be watching Kriti more closely now. And she was going to pay more attention to what Kriti was eating—or not eating! Or how much she was exercising—make that overexercising! If worse came to worst, she would speak to Grandmother about it.

6

NEW YORK DEBUT

"WHY ISN'T TAYLOR BACK YET?" demanded Eliza at breakfast on Wednesday. Grandmother had just excused herself to an early hair appointment, and Eliza seemed to be using this brief period of "freedom" to hammer on DJ again.

"Because she's not." DJ poured herself a second cup of coffee then added milk, stirring slowly.

"Where is she anyway?"

"I already told you." DJ frowned at her.

"Are you saying she's still in LA?"

DJ gave her a blank look as she sipped her coffee.

"Why is she there?" persisted Eliza.

"Because she is," said DJ.

Eliza turned to Rhiannon now. "How about you … do you know why Taylor's still gone or when she'll be back?"

"What difference does it make?" Rhiannon smiled as she reached for another piece of toast.

"How about you, Casey?" Eliza was trying a more persuasive voice now. "Maybe you know why Taylor is still down—"

"Maybe it's none of your business." Casey narrowed her eyes. "Why do you care so much anyway? It's not like you two are even friends."

"We *are* friends." Eliza looked at DJ now. "Tell them about how Taylor and I got along in Vegas. Were we or were we not friends then?"

"It depends on how you define friends. I'll admit you two have had some common interests." DJ sort of laughed. "Like drinking too much and wearing expensive clothes, and, oh yeah, guys. Or at least you had these things in the past. Maybe that's changing now."

Eliza glared at them. "Taylor Mitchell is as much my friend as she is to any of you all."

"Then, if you're so chummy with Taylor, why hasn't she called you and told you where she is and when she's coming back?" teased Casey.

"Why don't you just let it go?" suggested DJ. "She'll get here when she gets here."

"If she gets here," added Casey.

Eliza's eyes brightened. "Meaning she might be gone for good?"

"You'd like that, wouldn't you?" accused Casey. "If Taylor never came back, you'd think you were the hottest thing in Carter House."

Eliza gave Casey an icy look.

"Seriously, Eliza," said DJ with much more patience than she felt. "Why are you suddenly so obsessed over Taylor's whereabouts?"

Eliza looked indignant. "Because she happens to be my roommate."

Casey snickered. "Her stuff is in your room, Eliza. That's all. I seriously doubt that Taylor will ever willingly agree to be your roommate."

"Something is going on here," said Eliza with undisguised suspicion. "Taylor has gotten into some kind of trouble, and you guys are trying to cover for her. But I just know that something happened to Taylor. I can almost smell it."

"Give it a rest," warned DJ.

"No, I'm going to get to the bottom of this."

"Good luck," said Casey.

"I'll bet she's pregnant," said Eliza suddenly. "I'm going to ask Seth. He's been playing dumb too. But my guess is he—"

"She is *not* pregnant!" snapped DJ.

"Well, then she's in jail."

"She's not in jail either!" DJ stood now. "Please, *excuse* me."

"You seem to know where she's *not*, DJ," continued Eliza, "and that must mean you know where she *is*. I promise you, I'll find out."

"And I'll get her, my pretty . . ." Casey cackled like the Wicked Witch of the West. "And her little dog too!"

Everyone except Eliza and Kriti laughed as they all made an exodus from the breakfast table. This was followed by the usual last-minute get-ready-for-school rush, including much clomping up and down the stairs and the touching up of makeup as everyone got their bags and things and headed off to beat the bell.

"Why is Eliza so obsessed with finding out about Taylor?" asked Rhiannon as DJ backed out of the driveway so that Eliza could get out.

"I think Casey hit the nail on the head," said DJ. "Because Taylor is her main competition in the fashion show."

"It's not like it's a competitive event," said Rhiannon.

"Eliza acts like she's fighting to become America's Next Top Model," added Casey.

"Everything is a competition to Eliza." DJ watched as Eliza's Porsche zipped out, taking off ahead of them. "She has a need to be on top. And, no offense to you guys since I think you're both gorgeous, but Taylor is probably Eliza's biggest beauty rival."

"Yeah …" Rhiannon sighed. "I think Eliza is secretly hoping that Taylor doesn't come back at all."

"She doesn't have to be such a witch about it." Casey shook her fist at the back of Eliza's car.

"It's probably not helping that she's still in a snit over her house arrest," suggested Rhiannon.

"I have a feeling she's about to receive her get-out-of-jail-free card," admitted DJ. "My grandmother really does have a weak spot when it comes to beauty. Did you hear her complimenting Eliza on her hair and makeup this morning? I could see her softening up to Eliza already."

"I know," Casey agreed, "and it probably doesn't hurt when Eliza puts on her Miss Perfect Manners routine."

"At least when my grandmother is watching."

DJ turned into the school parking lot, quickly spotting a vacant space. "Hey, Rhiannon, can you get a ride home from school again tonight? Casey and I have a game."

"You can always ask dear, sweet Eliza for a ride," teased Casey.

Rhiannon frowned as they got out of the car. "I know Eliza has her problems … but I think we still need to love her."

"That's true, Rhiannon," admitted DJ. "I guess I just need to be reminded … a lot."

"I'll leave the loving Eliza thing up to you guys," said Casey. "I'll try to be a little more tolerant, but I can't promise anything."

As they walked toward school, DJ suddenly remembered her conversation with Kriti last night. "Oh, yeah!" she said "I almost forgot to tell you—we might need to do another intervention."

"What?" Rhiannon looked shocked. "Don't tell me that Eliza is—"

"Not Eliza," corrected DJ. "I mean Kriti. And this time it's not drugs or alcohol."

"Is she a secret gambler?" ventured Casey.

"No!" DJ couldn't help but chuckle to imagine little Kriti glued to a one-armed bandit. "Nothing like that."

"What then?"

So DJ quickly explained about Kriti's new obsession with weight loss—how she was overdoing the exercising and not eating. "She's totally convinced she is too fat!"

"No way!" Rhiannon cried. "She's so tiny."

"Eliza told her she should weigh less for her height. And now Kriti is freaked. I watched her at breakfast this morning, and she barely ate a bite of toast. I think she's starving herself."

"Poor Kriti." Rhiannon shook her head. "I guess we should've seen this one coming."

"I blame my grandmother partly," added DJ as they entered the school. "Her manic focus on low-fat, low-carb, low-taste foods ... well, it's no wonder Kriti has fallen into the gotta-be-skinny trap."

"So what do we do?"

"I'm not sure," admitted DJ. "But I wanted you guys to know so we could start thinking of some way to help her. She's totally miserable."

"I knew something was wrong. But I thought maybe she was sick or brokenhearted or something," said Casey. "She hasn't been herself for weeks now."

"Why don't we get together after your game," suggested Rhiannon, "and do some brainstorming."

"Sounds good," agreed Casey.

"I'll try to do some research in the meantime," said Rhiannon.

"Research?"

"Yeah. So we can bring some facts to the table for Kriti."

"Good idea," said DJ. "And maybe we can help her to see that exercise is healthy, but not the way she's doing it."

"I guess it was good that your grandmother moved her out of Eliza's room after all," said Rhiannon. "Who knew?"

"So . . . what did you find online?" DJ asked Rhiannon after dinner that night. The three of them had holed up in Casey and Rhiannon's room to figure out a way to help Kriti. Rhiannon actually made a list of their observations. 1) Kriti barely ate a bite at dinner, 2) she tried to appear to eat by moving her food around the plate and nibbling on mini bites of vegetables, and 3) she was clearly miserable. After dinner, the three of them had spied on her doing jumping jacks on the third floor—very vigorously too.

Rhiannon picked up what she'd printed from a website. "Well, she's most likely anorexic and not bulimic."

"What's the difference?" asked Casey. "I always thought they were kind of the same thing."

"Bulimics overeat and then purge."

"Purge?" Casey looked confused.

"You know, they barf." DJ made a disgusted face.

"Right, I knew that. But why not just call it barfing?"

"Well, there are other ways they purge too," explained Rhiannon. "They also use laxatives."

"Ugh." Now Casey made a face.

"But anorexics basically starve themselves," said Rhiannon. "They live on things like diet pop, rice cakes, green salads with no dressing, and—"

"That's almost exactly what Kriti has for lunch most days," said DJ. "A plain green salad, but she has iced tea, not soda. And I never see her adding sugar to it."

"Right." Rhiannon nodded. "But here's something else. These girls—the ones who become really seriously anorexic or bulimic—often develop a skewed body image."

"What do you mean?" asked DJ.

"There's actually a scientific name for it, but I can't remember it right now. Anyway, it's like these girls look at themselves in the mirror but instead of seeing what they actually look like, they see something totally different. One website described it like looking into those wavy carnival mirrors that make you look short and fat and weird."

"I think I saw something like that on TV," said Casey. "Like sometimes a woman thinks something's wrong with her face and even though everyone else tells her she looks great, she keeps getting plastic surgery until she doesn't even look human anymore."

"Yes," said Rhiannon. "I saw a woman who wanted to remake herself to look like a Barbie doll—she had like fifty plastic surgeries and ended up looking totally bizarre."

"But back to Kriti," said DJ.

"That seems kind of like what Kriti is doing," said Rhiannon. "Not the plastic surgery part, but the way she sees herself."

"Thinking she's fat," added Casey.

"Which is nuts," said DJ. "I mean, she has curves, but she is *not* fat."

"Apparently that's not how she sees herself." Rhiannon looked at Casey and DJ and sighed. "Although I kind of understand her perspective."

"What do you mean?" asked Casey.

69

"Well … you and DJ and Eliza and Taylor are all tall … and slender. It's like you four really do look like models. I might not be as short as Kriti, but I know how she feels in a way."

DJ punched a pillow. "I blame my grandmother for a lot of this. She makes such a big deal about modeling." She looked at Rhiannon. "But I always felt like you were pretty grounded."

"Yeah," agreed Casey. "You seem to have a good self-image."

"Maybe it *seems* that way, but believe me, I have plenty of insecurities."

"Like what?" demanded DJ.

"Like it's not easy being the poor girl."

DJ shook her head. "Hey, you might not have as much money, but you are wealthy when it comes to natural talent, Rhiannon."

"And wealthy when it comes to being a genuinely good person," added Casey.

Rhiannon smiled. "Thanks."

"Besides the fact that you're gorgeous," said DJ. "Even Grandmother has said—plenty of times—that you'd be a great print model."

"I just want to be a designer," said Rhiannon. "But we need to get back to Kriti."

"Yeah," said Casey. "What are we going to do?"

"For starters, we could try to convince her that she doesn't need to lose weight," said Rhiannon.

"Not that she'll listen," said DJ. "I mean, you should've heard her when I tried to point out that she was *not* fat. She couldn't hear me. It's like she's been brainwashed."

"In a way, she probably has." Rhiannon shook her head sadly. "Too many skinny images in movies, TV, and magazines. Don't we all get a little brainwashed?"

"Eliza always has a pile of fashion magazines in her room."

"Hey, do you think Eliza is anorexic too?" asked Casey.

"I think she *plays* with it," said DJ. "I know she counts calories and watches her carbs and fats."

"But she's not obsessed by it," added Rhiannon. "I mean, we've all seen her eat. She's not a pig, but she's not starving herself either."

"And she seems pretty pleased with how she looks," said DJ.

"Why shouldn't she be?" Rhiannon sighed. "She's beautiful."

"And she wants everyone to notice too." Casey scowled.

"Okay, we're not here to bash Eliza," Rhiannon reminded them.

"So what's our plan for Kriti?" asked DJ.

"Well, I think your idea for an intervention was the perfect answer," Rhiannon told her. "We just need to figure out how to do it."

"You ever get the feeling we're running some kind of clinic here?" joked DJ. "Like maybe my grandmother should switch her focus from fashion to mental health. We could be the Carter House Rehabilitation Center for Young Women."

They all laughed, but DJ actually thought it was sort of pathetic. She also thought that her grandmother should bear some of the blame if the girls under her care got any more messed up. Oh, sure, maybe these things would've happened anyway. But maybe not this latest problem with Kriti. It seemed a direct result of the atmosphere in this house. Not that Grandmother would be that concerned to hear about it.

"So how do we intervene?" asked Casey. "Like you did with me when I was stealing DJ's pain pills? Remember how you cornered me in my room and went into attack mode?"

"We didn't attack you."

"That's what it felt like."

"Do you wish we hadn't intervened?"

"No, not at all. But it sure wasn't easy at the time." Casey's expression grew serious. "Now it's hard to believe that I really did what I did. Not to mention embarrassing. I honestly don't believe I would ever do anything like that again—although my counselor still reminds me not to let my guard down."

"Let's hope you don't."

"I'm still doing my counseling," said Casey quickly. "I've committed to go twice a month until the end of the school year."

"Cool," said DJ. "Now back to Kriti. What's next?"

"We agree she needs to be confronted."

"And we need to be honest and direct with her," said Rhiannon, "but with kindness and love. She needs to know we really care about her."

"And we've got to make her see that she's not fat," added DJ. "Or at least we have to try."

"Plus we need to attach some consequences," said Casey. "Like the way you guys did with me. Otherwise, it's like the intervention has no teeth."

They all thought about this, and then DJ spoke. "The consequence will be that I'll inform my grandmother, and she will inform Kriti's parents."

"Yes!" said Casey and Rhiannon simultaneously.

"The question is *when?*" said DJ.

"There's no time like the present," said Casey. "I mean, why put it off?"

"The sooner we can help her, the sooner she can get better." Rhiannon held up another sheet of paper. "I printed out a list of all these horrible side effects. We may need to read it to her."

"Good thinking," said DJ. "Kriti's smart. She respects facts."

"Okay," said Rhiannon. "We should do the same thing we did before our intervention with Casey."

"What?" asked Casey.

"Pray."

Casey frowned. "Do you expect me to believe Taylor prayed too?"

"She did her part," said DJ.

"So can Casey," added Rhiannon. Then she led them in a prayer for Kriti. They asked God to give them the right words, and they prayed that Kriti would be able hear what they were saying. "Mostly, dear God," prayed Rhiannon finally, "help Kriti to know that we love her and care about her. Amen."

"Ready?" asked DJ.

"All for one, and one for all?" Casey made a goofy face.

"Yeah, I guess that works."

By now Kriti had returned to her room. She was sitting on her bed, but still breathing hard, and her cheeks were flushed from her ridiculous exercise regime.

"Hey," said DJ as the three girls entered the room. "Can we talk to you?"

"Me?" Kriti looked up in surprise.

"Yeah," said Rhiannon.

Kriti shrugged. "What's going on?"

"Let's all sit down," DJ said. Then she and the others sat across from Kriti on the edge of DJ's bed.

"Here's the deal," began DJ. "We're worried about you."

Kriti frowned. "Well, don't be."

"We can't help it," said Rhiannon. "We think you're in trouble."

"Trouble?" Kriti looked skeptical. "What are you talking about?"

"We think you're becoming anorexic."

Now this seemed to catch Kriti off guard. But instead of defending herself, she just waved her hand, as if to brush it off. "That's ludicrous."

"Not really," said DJ. "We all know you're not eating. We all know you're overexercising. And I know, based on what you told me, that you are seeing yourself all wrong."

Kriti's dark brows drew closer together, but she said nothing.

"You have a skewed body image," added Rhiannon. "It's no wonder, after living with Eliza the past five months. She's so obsessed with being thin and beautiful, and she's got all those magazines, and you were—"

"It seems a little unfair to blame Eliza for my behavior." Kriti's lower jaw jutted out ever so slightly.

"So you admit that there's a problem with your behavior?" asked DJ.

"Like I already told you, I'm trying to take off a few pounds."

"Why?" asked Rhiannon.

"Duh." Kriti poked her midsection. "Isn't it obvious?"

"No!" they all declared at once.

"You guys are just trying to be nice ... well, in a *mean* sort of way."

"Mean?" Casey frowned. "We're just trying to help you."

"I do *not* need your help."

"So you deny that you're anorexic?" asked DJ.

Kriti nodded firmly. "That's right."

"Okay, maybe that's good," said DJ. "You're not officially anorexic yet, but you're in anorexic training camp."

Kriti looked down at her lap without speaking.

"Do you have any idea of what anorexia can do to a person?" asked Rhiannon. Before Kriti could answer, Rhiannon began to read from the list. "Malnutrition can permanently harm your bones and stunt your growth, not just your weight, but your height too. It can ruin your hair and nails, and your hair could fall out. Eventually your skin gets all dried out, and you turn yellow. You might break out or get patchy blotches and you will — "

"That's enough!" Kriti held her hands up to stop her.

"Not quite," said Rhiannon. "Anorexia also messes with your vital organs. It can cause your heart to stop and — "

"I said to *stop*." Kriti stood now. With her hands on her hips, she glared at the three of them. "Just leave me alone."

Rhiannon shoved the list toward Kriti. "You're a smart girl, Kriti. Read through this stuff yourself if you don't believe me."

Kriti tossed the papers on her bed.

"Here's the deal, Kriti," began DJ in a more gentle tone. "We really care about you. And we can all see that you do *not* need to lose a single pound." DJ stood up now, gently but firmly pushing Kriti over to the full-length mirror on the closet door. "Look at yourself, Kriti. *You are not fat.*"

Kriti looked but just shook her head in unbelief.

"You want to see fat?" said Casey as she stood and pulled off her shirt, standing in front of Kriti in her bra. "Look at this belly." Then she reached down and pinched at some midsection flab.

"Yeah," said DJ as she pulled Kriti into the bathroom where the mirror was larger and peeled off her own shirt, "Look at this."

Soon all three of them had their shirts off. They all stood in front of the wide bathroom mirror and poked fun at various parts of their bodies.

"No one looks like those airbrushed models in the magazines," said Rhiannon.

"Not even the models," pointed out DJ.

"Yeah, I've heard they do all kinds of computerized tricks to make them look better," added Casey.

"But, here's the deal." DJ slapped her own rear end that she'd just been making fun of and calling her *junk in the trunk*. "I'm okay with how I look."

"Me too," added Rhiannon. She pointed to her chest, which she'd just admitted could barely fill an A cup. "And I'm not getting implants either."

"Take off your shirt," Casey urged Kriti.

She just shook her head.

"Sure, you let us all stand here showing you how picture perfect we aren't. Then you refuse to play. Nice!" Casey frowned at Kriti.

"Fine." Kriti slowly unbuttoned and then took off her shirt.

"Look at you," said Rhiannon. "You're the skinniest girl in the mirror."

Kriti frowned and looked down at herself. "No, I'm not."

"You are too!" insisted DJ. "Look at yourself. Look at us. It's obvious."

Kriti looked back at her reflection now, squinting as if her eyes hurt.

"Do we need to take a photo to prove it?" asked Casey. "I'm willing to get my camera."

"Want me to go get my measuring tape?" asked Rhiannon.

But Kriti's expression changed ever so slightly as she stared into the mirror, trying to see what they saw.

"Are you seeing it yet?" demanded DJ.

"I don't know."

"Do you want us to stand here all night until you get it?" asked Casey.

"Or maybe we should strip naked," said DJ. "Would that help?"

Kriti sort of giggled now. "No, not really. But thanks for the offer."

"Okay," said Rhiannon as she pulled her shirt back on.

Soon they were in the bedroom again, and DJ felt it was time to give the ultimatum. "Look, Kriti," she began slowly. "Because we all really care about you, we want you to stop this. Do you get that?"

Kriti nodded solemnly.

"And it's possible you might need help," said Rhiannon. "The article I gave you says that if a case goes on too long, the patient might need both medical and psychological treatment."

Now Kriti looked truly alarmed.

"But that might not be how it is with you," said DJ quickly. "For starters we'll give you the benefit of the doubt. Okay?"

She looked relieved.

"But here's the deal," continued DJ. "You *have* to start eating. And you have to stop that manic exercising. I mean, it's great if you want to work out. There's nothing wrong with good exercise, and Casey and I can even help you with a sensible workout program."

Kriti looked slightly interested, then she frowned. "But what if I don't want your help? What if I refuse to ... well, to change?"

"That's what I'm getting to." DJ took in a deep breath. "If you refuse our help and keep doing what you've been doing, I *will* tell my grandmother everything. And she will inform your parents so that they can deal with it. I'm guessing they'll move you back home."

"But we'd really like you to stick around," added Rhiannon.

"Really?" Kriti did not look convinced.

"Okay. We realize we haven't been that friendly. But that's mostly because Eliza seemed to rule over you."

"Yeah, it's like you became her personal property," said Casey.

Kriti nodded like she got this. "I guess it kind of felt that way to me too. Still, she's nice in her own way. And she seems to care about me. And she's so beautiful. Eliza was the first real friend I've had."

"*Real* friend?" DJ studied Kriti closely. "Do you really believe that?"

"I don't know ..."

"Don't you feel like she kind of uses you?" asked Rhiannon. "I mean, it seems like you do everything for her ... but what does she do for you?"

"Besides telling you that you're fat?" said Casey.

Kriti slowly nodded. "Okay ... maybe you're right."

"Look," said DJ. "You are smart and pretty, and you really have a lot going on. You don't need to be someone's puppet."

Kriti gave them a half smile.

"So, are you going to cooperate with us?" asked Casey.

"Because we'll be watching you closely," said Rhiannon. "Both here and at school."

"We're going to be keeping track of whether or not you're really eating," said Casey.

"And I'll be watching to make sure you don't overexercise."

"It's just because we want to help," added Rhiannon. "We want you to be healthy."

"Are you in?" asked DJ. "Will you cooperate?"

"Yes." Kriti nodded as if she meant it. "I will."

DJ grinned. "Okay, here's your first test. I'm hungry for a hot fudge sundae. Who's ready to go with me?"

"And fries too?" asked Kriti.

"I KNOW WHERE TAYLOR IS," chirped Eliza on Saturday morning.

The girls were at the breakfast table, but Grandmother had been delayed with a phone call so the conversation was fairly relaxed. "Where?" DJ asked, trying to sound disinterested.

"Rehab," said Eliza proudly.

"Says who?" DJ was still trying to act nonchalant as she applied the butter substitute to her whole-grain toast.

"Says Seth."

"How would Seth know?" asked Casey.

"He happens to be Taylor's boyfriend." Eliza dabbed her lips with a napkin. "Why wouldn't he know?"

"Why would he tell you?" demanded DJ.

"Because I know how to get what I want from a guy." Eliza smiled smugly.

"Maybe he lied to you," suggested Casey.

Eliza laughed. "Look, I don't see why you guys are trying to cover for Taylor. We all know she has a drinking problem. You should be glad she's getting treatment. How long is she in for, DJ?"

DJ took a big bite of her toast and slowly chewed. She was determined not to engage with Eliza.

"Just because Seth said that Taylor is in rehab doesn't make it true," persisted Casey. "How would he even know ... I mean, I've heard that people aren't allowed contact with the outside world when they're in rehab."

"He said that Taylor called him."

"Taylor called him?" demanded DJ with her mouth still partially full of toast.

"Ah-ha!" Eliza looked pleased, kind of like the spider that just caught the fly. "So she really is in rehab."

"I didn't say that."

"You don't need to, DJ. Your face says it all. I actually thought that Seth was just making it up. But now I know that he was telling the truth after all."

"Whatever." DJ rolled her eyes, but inwardly simmered to think that Taylor had called Seth and not her.

"Are we all ready for our modeling class?" asked Eliza cheerfully. "This is the big day when the other girls start coming."

"Don't remind us." Casey groaned. "I can't believe we're being forced to spend the next few Saturday mornings with people like Madison and Tina."

"I doubt that Madison and Tina will really come," said DJ. "I'll bet they were kidding."

"Why wouldn't they want to come?" asked Eliza. "It's a great opportunity for girls outside of Carter House to improve themselves." She gave DJ a catty smile now. "I know a couple girls right under this roof who could use some improvements as well."

DJ didn't respond. She simply excused herself. Why did Eliza make life so difficult? And this news about Taylor calling Seth was especially aggravating. After all DJ had done for Taylor ... and then Taylor calls stupid Seth instead of her. Seth, who'd been arrested for underage drinking himself. She wondered if Seth had told Taylor about that little incident.

DJ went to her room and flopped onto her bed. She had to agree with Casey ... the last thing she wanted to do this morning was to sit in a room with girls like Madison and Tina, not to mention Eliza, and to be forced to listen as Grandmother droned on about the correct care of cuticles or the necessity of weekly exfoliating masques or how to sit like you had a corncob stuck in some hidden part of your anatomy. Or, puh-leeze, how to walk. DJ knew how to walk. She just wished she could walk out.

"Is it true about Taylor?" asked Kriti as she came into the room.

DJ shrugged. "I guess the cat's out of the bag now."

"Well, I think it's a good thing."

"You mean that she's in rehab? Or that everyone knows?"

"That she's getting help."

"Yeah, I have to agree with you there." DJ gave her a little smile now. "By the way, good job at breakfast. I noticed you ate all your oatmeal." Okay, DJ didn't mention that the bowl had only been half full. But at least Kriti had polished it off.

Kriti nodded with an uncertain expression and then went to look in the full-length mirror and scowled at her reflection.

"Don't obsess," DJ reminded as she got up and went to stand beside Kriti. "Or I'll have to hang sheets over all the mirrors."

Kriti sighed, then went to the bathroom and picked up her brush, going to work on her shoulder-length black hair, although it seemed that every hair was already in perfect place. "So when is Taylor coming back?" asked Kriti as she set the brush down.

"I have no idea." DJ leaned forward and peered at her own reflection. No makeup. Straggly hair in need of a wash. Old soccer shirt and comfy jeans. Comfy, but not too impressive—especially to her grandmother. Not that DJ particularly cared.

"Taylor will probably want her room back ... I mean, here with you."

DJ shrugged. "I don't know."

"Well, I cannot imagine that she'll want to share a room with Eliza."

DJ laughed. "I can't imagine *anyone* wanting to share a room with Eliza. I mean, she hogs the closet space, acts like she thinks she's the perfect princess, and makes the rest of us feel like the ugly stepsisters."

"You too?" Kriti was putting on some blush now. Grandmother had told them to come to class looking their best. Apparently Kriti had been listening.

DJ nodded. "Oh, yeah. Not only that, but she's so graceful, she makes me feel like a klutz with two left feet."

"Me too." Kriti was putting on lip color. "Did you know that she took ballet for six years?"

"Why does that not surprise me?" DJ sighed.

"And piano too."

"The perfect little princess." Of course, DJ felt guilty now. What about all that talk of loving her enemies? To be fair, Eliza wasn't exactly an enemy. It wasn't like she'd done anything specifically mean or horrid to DJ. At least not recently. Although DJ hadn't forgotten how Eliza had tripped her at the last fashion show.

"I think it might've helped when Taylor was here," said Kriti.

"Huh?"

"Taylor sort of balanced out the power with Eliza." Kriti expertly brushed some blusher onto her cheeks, probably just the way Eliza had taught her to do. Still, it looked nice and natural too.

"I think you're right."

"Do you miss Taylor?" Kriti looked directly at DJ now.

DJ wasn't quite sure how to answer. She didn't want to lie, but telling the truth might make Kriti feel bad since she was in essence sleeping in Taylor's bed. "I sort of miss her, but I'm glad she's getting help too."

"You felt bad that she didn't call you, didn't you?"

"Yeah."

"And you were keeping her rehab a secret to protect her?"

"It seemed like she should be the one to tell people . . . that is, if she wanted."

"You're a good friend, DJ."

"Thanks." DJ pulled her hair into a messy ponytail now. She knew Grandmother would not be pleased with her appearance. But that was her problem. Maybe Grandmother would dismiss her from practice—now wouldn't that be nice. Or maybe DJ might get really lucky and her grandmother would choose someone like Madison or Tina to take DJ's place for Fashion Week.

"As you girls all know, I have decided to take eight models with me to Fashion Week." Grandmother looked over what appeared to be about a dozen girls and smiled. "Not that I want you girls to think of this as a competition. It is certainly not. Because we're all here to learn, aren't we? So even if you're not one of the lucky eight who goes to New York, you will leave Carter House knowing that you are prettier and more charming and better groomed than when you came."

It took all of DJ's self-control not to moan as Grandmother continued. It seemed that the main topic of today's "lesson" was about clothing and styles. Like DJ cared.

"Vertical lines make you appear taller and thinner," explained Grandmother as she showed them a photo of a tall, skinny model wearing a black and white striped dress with stripes going up and down. Personally, DJ thought the model looked stupid. And the hungry-looking girl was already tall and thin. Like, how much taller and thinner did she need to look? Then Grandmother produced another photo of a shorter, stockier girl — obviously not a model — wearing black and white stripes that went from side to side and caused her to resemble a prison inmate.

"You can see how these horizontal stripes make her look dumpy and fat." Grandmother made a *tsk-tsk* sound. "A fashion disaster."

DJ felt herself nodding off, and she tried to fight it. But suddenly she was brought back to consciousness by a nudge from Casey's elbow.

"Huh?" muttered DJ.

"Your grandmother," whispered Casey.

DJ looked up to see Grandmother sternly looking her direction. "I *said*, please, come up here, Desiree."

DJ kind of shrugged, then stood and shuffled forward. Grandmother cleared her throat, then shook her head. "As I was saying, there are many fashion don'ts. It seems that my own granddaughter has decided to demonstrate most of them for us today." This elicited some chuckles from the girls.

DJ forced a grin. "Thank you very much."

"Stand up straight, dear."

DJ straightened.

"Now. For starters, Desiree's hair is all wrong. Pulled back like this only accentuates her rather long face and square chin."

DJ touched her chin. It didn't feel square.

"And her lack of makeup makes her skin look sallow." Grandmother pointed below her eyes. "And see these bags."

"Bags?" DJ turned and stared at Grandmother.

"Yes. A little properly applied concealer will take care of that. But I'm digressing. I only brought her up here to talk about her clothing, to show how color and style can work for you or against you." She pulled at DJ's baggy shirt with a broad stripe across the chest. "Now this shirt adds about ten pounds to Desiree. The blue stripe accentuates her bust line, but not in a flattering way. The sagging shoulders make it appear that she is slouching." Grandmother frowned. "Usually she is slouching. But beneath this ill-fitting shirt, Desiree actually has very nice, straight shoulders. Not that anyone can see that today. And she also has a very trim figure. But you wouldn't know that to look at her. And these jeans." Grandmother shook her head hopelessly as she tugged at them. "They do not accentuate anything worth accentuating. In fact, these jeans really should be burned."

"I like them," said DJ. "They're comfy."

Grandmother laughed. "Comfort and fashion have very little to do with one another, dear."

Madison snickered loudly, causing Tina to break into giggles. But Grandmother didn't even look their way. Instead, she continued to go over all of DJ's numerous "fashion don'ts." As Grandmother continued to point out the poorly positioned back pockets of DJ's must-be-burned, drooping jeans, DJ stared directly at Madison, watching the smug girl sit there with one leg crossed over the other, swinging her foot and smiling in a superior way.

Finally, Grandmother seemed to run out of negative things to say about DJ, and she invited Eliza to come and stand next to her.

"Eliza will be our *good* example," said Grandmother. Like she needed to explain that. Then she went over all of Eliza's "fashion do's" and compared them to DJ's "don'ts." Once again, Madison and Tina seemed to enjoy DJ's discomfort thoroughly. But DJ just stood there, gritting her teeth and taking it. She wished she was thinking more Christ-like thoughts, but mostly she wanted to smack Madison right in the nose.

"Lesson learned," DJ admitted to Casey later. "Next Saturday I'll take a bit more care with my appearance. That way I might be able to sleep while Grandmother picks on some other poor unsuspecting soul."

"Like me?" Casey frowned.

"Be warned."

On Sunday, after Conner drove DJ home from church, Taylor called. Fortunately, Kriti was gone, so DJ was able to talk privately in her room.

"How *are* you?" she asked happily.

"Pretty good."

"So you're allowed to use the phone?"

"This is my very first call."

"Oh?" DJ didn't want to contradict Taylor, but she was curious. "I, uh, I heard you called Seth."

"Yeah, like weeks ago."

"When?"

"Before I signed myself into lockdown."

"Oh ..." Now DJ felt bad for questioning her, but she was curious. "But Seth did know where you were then?"

"Sort of."

"Because I was trying to keep it quiet, I figured you didn't want everyone to know what was going on."

"Are you saying that everyone knows now?" Taylor sounded mad.

"They didn't hear it from me."

"And I told Seth to keep his mouth shut."

"He did for the most part. But somehow Eliza pried it out of him."

Taylor swore.

"I'm sorry," DJ said quickly. "I just found out this morning. Up until now, it's been top secret. Unfortunately, Eliza announced it to everyone at breakfast." Okay, DJ didn't admit that she had told Rhiannon and Casey. But, unlike Big Mouth Eliza, they had kept it to themselves. Plus, Rhiannon, like DJ, had been praying for Taylor, and DJ felt that was worth a lot.

"Oh, I guess it doesn't really matter anyway." Taylor sighed loudly.

"If it makes you feel any better, everyone here—well, except Eliza—thinks it's pretty cool." Then to change the subject, DJ told Taylor about their Saturday sessions in preparation for Fashion Week and how Grandmother had invited outsiders and how she'd used DJ as her "don't" example.

Taylor laughed. "You should've known better, DJ."

"Yeah, well, I won't make that mistake again."

"I suppose Eliza thinks she's the Carter House fashion queen now."

So DJ told Taylor about Eliza's New Year's Eve party, including how Eliza, Harry, and Seth had all been arrested.

"No way!" Taylor was laughing really hard now. "Wow, that just makes my day. Eliza in jail?"

"I'm not sure if she was really locked up. But she did get caught. She had to clean the whole house, including scrubbing toilets. Plus she's been grounded all week. Although I suspect it's about over now. Eliza's been buttering up my grandmother with her southern charm and impeccable manners."

"That girl is so sweet that sugar wouldn't melt in her mouth."

DJ laughed. "I miss you!"

"You know, I miss you too."

"When are you coming back?"

"Good question."

"Do you have a good answer?"

"Well, it's sort of up to me."

"Meaning they'll let you out now?"

"Well . . . I think I might still need another week or two."

"Will you be back in time for Fashion Week?"

"That's the plan. But here's the deal, okay?"

"What?"

"Don't tell anyone I'm coming back yet."

"Why not?"

"Because I think it'll be fun to make a big appearance. Kind of dramatic, you know."

"When will you get here?"

"In time . . . just in the nick of time."

"In time for New York, right?"

"For sure!"

"Because my grandmother is really worried that you won't be back in time for the big New York debut," said DJ. "In fact, she still kind of blames me that you're gone now."

"That's a little harsh."

"Tell me about it."

"Well, don't worry, and don't tell her, but I will be there—with bells on." She laughed. "Okay, maybe not the bell part. But I will be there!"

"I love it." To be honest, what DJ probably loved best was that Taylor's surprise appearance would put Eliza in her place. And, fine, it was one thing to love your enemies, but was it wrong to want them to get what was coming to them? Anyway, DJ would have to figure that one out later.

"Promise me, DJ, mum's the word, okay?"

"Absolutely." But this time DJ knew she would tell no one. Not even Rhiannon or Casey. "And you're sure you don't want to let my grandmother know you'll be back in time for New York?"

"I don't see why."

Come to think of it, DJ didn't either. As long as Taylor got back in time, there wasn't a chance that she shouldn't be in the show. Because, as far as Grandmother was concerned, Taylor *was* the show. Okay, Taylor and Eliza were both fashion stars. But Taylor was still in first place. After that was anyone's guess.

"Well, I'm supposed to limit this call to five minutes."

"Hey, what about Seth?"

Taylor let out a growl. "Tell that boy *nothing*."

"You got it."

"I'll deal with him when I get back."

DJ chuckled. "Well, it's really good to hear your voice. You take care now."

"You too. Don't let Eliza walk all over you."

"Like there's a way to avoid it?"

"There will be," said Taylor, "when I get back."

DJ laughed, then told Taylor good-bye. But after she shut her phone, she wished she'd told Taylor that she loved her. Except that it sounded so weird. But the truth was DJ did love Taylor. That's when it occurred to her — Taylor used to be DJ's worst enemy! She used to totally hate her. So maybe it was possible to love your enemies.

8

NEW YORK DEBUT

"DO YOU KNOW THAT MADISON is telling everyone that she's going to New York to model in Fashion Week?" said Casey as DJ joined her friends at lunch.

"What?"

"Eliza was just telling us."

"That's right," Eliza said importantly. "I actually heard Madison bragging about it to someone in the restroom a few minutes ago."

"Did you set her straight?" asked DJ.

"Not yet." Eliza grinned mischievously. "But we will."

"But how do you know she's not going to be in the show?" asked Rhiannon. "Mrs. Carter already said she's taking eight girls. And even if she took all five of us from the house, which she hasn't promised, that still leaves three spots to fill."

DJ wanted to correct her and say "two spots," but stopped herself. No one was supposed to know that Taylor was coming back yet.

"Madison probably has as good a chance as anyone," admitted Casey.

"Plus she was really buttering up Mrs. Carter," pointed out Rhiannon.

"She did seem highly motivated," added Kriti. "I watched her practicing the walk, and she was really focused."

"Puh-leeze," said Eliza. "Do not suggest that Mrs. Carter would choose Madison. Seriously, that will ruin everything."

"I have to agree with Eliza on this," said Casey. "Having Madison in New York would be messed up. I'd think of an excuse not to go."

"You'd let someone like Madison squeeze you out of Fashion Week?" Eliza looked incredulous.

"Well, she's about the meanest girl I know. Have you guys ever seen her MySpace blog?"

"Why would we look at that?" Eliza turned her nose up like she smelled something bad.

"Because she slams all of us on it?" Casey scowled darkly. "If I hadn't promised never to use the Internet for, well, certain purposes, I'd get back at her for being such an online skank."

"Don't go there," warned DJ.

"I just said I wouldn't." Casey shook her head. "But I wish someone would."

"Why stoop to her level?" asked Rhiannon.

"If you knew what she said about us, you might understand."

"Let it go, Casey," said DJ.

"Yes," said Eliza. "Madison's so not worth it."

"I still remember the time she picked on me," said Kriti. "Right here at this table."

"I remember it too," said DJ.

"All that may be true about Madison," said Rhiannon. "But that doesn't mean Mrs. Carter won't choose her. She doesn't know what Madison is really like."

"I actually heard Mrs. Carter complimenting Madison on Saturday." Casey rolled her eyes. "I tried not to gag."

"And she *is* tall . . ."

"And some people, including Madison herself, think she's good-looking," added Casey.

"So, we just have to come up with a way to keep Madison out of the final lineup," Eliza said quietly.

"What can anyone do?" Kriti dipped a fry in ketchup, then popped it into her mouth. It was good to see her eating normally again—and smiling too. Also, she'd switched her class schedule to take Personal Training along with DJ in first period. "That way you can eat more," DJ had promised her.

"We need to do whatever it takes to make sure that the other girls stand out more than Madison," continued Eliza.

"How?" Casey asked her.

"We'll groom them ourselves."

DJ frowned. "We? As in all of us?"

Eliza laughed. "Well, some of us are better suited than others for this kind of project."

"Meaning I'm off the hook?"

Eliza studied DJ. "Not completely."

"Why?"

"You need to bring in some more girls with model potential."

"Huh?"

"You and Casey are on the basketball team. There must be some tall, thin girls there."

"Grandmother isn't only interested in tall, thin girls," said DJ, careful not to look at Kriti.

"That's right," said Rhiannon. "Take me for instance."

"Yes. But I want girls who will be shoo-ins."

"I think your grandmother likes Haley," continued Eliza. "We'll help to make sure she gets a spot. But we still need two more."

"What about Ariel Buford," suggested Rhiannon. "She's already taking the sessions, and Mrs. Carter seems to like her."

"She likes her because Ariel's grandmother is one of Grandmother's best friends," pointed out DJ.

"Meaning she'll probably make the cut anyway?" asked Casey.

"Probably," admitted DJ. "But she'll have to prove herself too."

Eliza seemed to consider this. "She's kind of mousy, but I suppose that could change. She did a good job on the catwalk."

"And she's pretty nice," said Casey.

"Okay. Ariel and Haley are on our list. But who else? We need at least one more."

DJ frowned. "It seems kind of wrong ... I mean, to be hand-picking girls like this."

"Do you want to share a room with Madison in New York?" demanded Eliza.

DJ grimaced. "Not especially."

"Okay, so we agree on Haley and Ariel." Eliza turned back to DJ. "You and Casey come up with a third girl. Someone with real model potential."

"What if no one is interested?"

Eliza laughed. "Don't be ridiculous. A free trip to New York?"

"Who says it's free?" questioned DJ.

"I'll pay the girl's way, okay? And I'll cover her session fees too. And I'll even give her a free makeover. What girl could resist all that?"

"Me." DJ pointed to herself, and everyone laughed.

"Just bring me someone I can work with," commanded Queen Eliza.

"Yeah, yeah." DJ rolled her eyes.

But later that day, as DJ and Casey were getting dressed after basketball practice, DJ noticed one of her friends from swim team—Daisy Kempton. DJ tried not to be too obvious as she watched Daisy zipping her jeans. Her hair was long and straggly, pulled back into a muddy-brown ponytail. Also, her complexion wasn't that great, and she was even more clueless about makeup than DJ had once been. Not only that, but Daisy was totally gawky and clumsy. She usually had two left feet on the basketball court. If it wasn't for her height and ability to stay planted near the basket, she would probably never get to play at all. Even today, she had fallen flat on her face while dribbling down court. DJ could relate to feeling clumsy sometimes, especially compared to Eliza or when she was on the catwalk. But for DJ it all changed when it came to sports. DJ was fairly coordinated and had even been called graceful before.

DJ nudged Casey. "Hey, how about Daisy?"

"She's tall and thin," observed Casey. "But she needs serious help."

"Be nice," said DJ.

"I'm just being honest."

They both watched as Daisy pulled her baggie sports sweatshirt over her head. She wasn't exactly the epitome of fashion. Not that DJ could talk, but at least she took a little more care in dressing for school. Daisy didn't seem to have a clue. Still, she was tall and thin. And it would be fun to see what Eliza could do with her.

"Let's talk to her about it," suggested DJ.

Casey frowned as she peered across the steamy dressing room to where Daisy was now shoving sweats into a messy locker. "Seriously?"

"Why not?"

"I'm not seeing it, DJ."

"Maybe not . . . but it would be fun to see what Eliza could do with her."

Casey chuckled "That's true."

"I just hope Eliza isn't mean to her." DJ watched as Daisy split her raggedy ponytail in two and pulled it with both hands to tighten it. Not a particularly good look.

"Poor Daisy." Casey shook her head. "Are you sure we should do this to her?"

"Come on." DJ grabbed Casey's arm and tugged her toward Daisy. "Hey, Daisy," she called out. "Wait a minute."

"What's up?" asked Daisy innocently.

"Have you ever considered modeling?"

Daisy laughed so hard that she actually snorted. "Me, a model? Are you kidding?"

"No," DJ answered quickly. "You've got the height for it."

"And you're thin," added Casey.

Daisy made a puzzled face. "You guys are pulling my leg, huh?"

"Not at all." Then DJ quickly told her about the Saturday sessions and Eliza's offer to pay her fees and give her a makeover.

"You're not serious."

"Totally."

Now Daisy looked suspicious "Hey, what's going on here? Are you guys punking me or something?"

"No way." DJ held up her hand like an oath. "Honestly."

"Why then?"

"Can we trust you?" asked DJ.

"I think the question is can I trust you?" Daisy glanced from DJ to Casey then back again.

"Do you have a few minutes?"

Daisy looked at her watch. "Not really. I'll miss the activities bus."

"I can give you a ride."

Daisy nodded. "Okay."

They stopped to get sodas on their way home, and DJ explained Eliza's plan. "You see, we really don't get along that well with Madison and Tina, and if we don't do something, they might end up going to New York."

"I don't get along with Madison and Tina either," admitted Daisy. "But I seriously don't see how I could possibly edge out either of those girls as a model. I mean ... have you looked at me? Get real."

"We are getting real," said Casey. "You actually have the right ingredients."

DJ grinned. "You just need a little help with the recipe."

"And Eliza *wants* to help," added Casey.

"Wow ... Eliza is so beautiful ..." Daisy shook her head in disbelief. "I can't imagine someone like her giving someone like me the time of day."

"Not only will she give you the time, she'll give you a great makeover too. She promised."

"And the sessions my grandmother teaches are supposed to help girls to learn poise and things," added DJ. Okay, she felt slightly hypocritical just then, but if anyone could use a little poise training ...

Daisy laughed. "I'm such a klutz. Do you really think she could help me?"

"If anyone can teach you grace, it would be Mrs. Carter," Casey assured her. "Not that it'll be easy."

Daisy nodded as if taking this all in.

"So ... are you interested?" DJ asked hopefully.

"I guess so." Daisy frowned now. "As long as you two swear this is not a punk and there are no hidden cameras involved. I mean, I have enough humiliation in my life without anyone helping me out."

"We promise this is not a punk."

"But what if I'm not good enough? What if I fail?"

"It'll be mostly up to Eliza," said DJ. "She's sure that if we bring her the raw materials, she can make a masterpiece."

"Well, I'm pretty raw." Daisy did her snort laugh again.

"Most importantly," said Casey, "you're nice."

"Thanks."

"And hopefully, you'll be just what we need to keep Madison and Tina from the starting lineup," said Casey.

Daisy chuckled. "I can just imagine those two as bench-warmers. They're not going to like it."

Once again, DJ felt slightly guilty. Was it unfair that the Carter House girls were trying to manipulate Grandmother's final cut? Or was it merely a matter of survival? Who could possibly survive the torture that it would bring if Tina and Madison were included in their group for Fashion Week? Sure, DJ knew she was supposed to love her enemies. And she'd been trying harder with Eliza. But when it came to Madison and Tina ... well, that was a whole different challenge. Why did there have to be so many enemies anyway?

9

NEW YORK DEBUT

ELIZA DIDN'T SAY ANYTHING when Casey and DJ first presented Daisy to her on Thursday evening. Her expression was impossible to read, although DJ was certain that she saw her flinch ever so slightly when Daisy wiped her nose on her sweatshirt sleeve. But at least Eliza didn't say anything mean or rude. Maybe there was something to those precious southern manners after all.

DJ glanced over to Kriti, who was quietly sitting on what used to be her bed. Eliza had asked all the Carter House girls to participate in this evening's makeover project. Although DJ wasn't too sure it was a good idea. She wasn't too sure that Daisy would appreciate being observed by them.

Eliza's plan was to introduce Daisy to Mrs. Carter and to beg for Daisy to be included in the model training. This might be tricky since there were only two sessions left before Fashion Week.

"We'll just have to convince your grandmother that it's an act of mercy," Eliza quietly told them while Daisy was using the bathroom. "We'll tell her that Daisy is our good friend, and she really needs someone like Mrs. Carter to take her under her wing. Okay?"

They all agreed, but DJ still wasn't so sure that Grandmother would buy this. Grandmother didn't like it when someone else attempted to usurp her power and control. But maybe Eliza knew how to pull it off with her sugary sweet charm. Besides, this was Eliza's plan, not DJ's. And if the plan blew up in Eliza's face, why should DJ care? Except that she did. Plus she felt like an accomplice now. Why couldn't life just be simple?

Eliza sighed. "Well, I certainly have my work cut out for me."

Casey laughed. "It might take a miracle."

"Or magic," said Eliza.

Casey had been hovering by the door and was suddenly reaching for the doorknob. "I'd stick around to see the fun and games, but I have homework tonight. Besides, it seems a little crowded in here."

"Maybe I'll go too," said DJ.

"Not so fast, DJ," commanded Eliza. "I might need you."

Eliza pointed to Casey now. "Send Rhiannon in. She promised to help me."

"Yes, your highness," teased Casey as she closed the door behind her.

"This is going to be a major challenge." Eliza was studying herself in the mirror now, smiling smugly as if perfectly pleased with her reflection. And why wouldn't she be? Except that beauty was only skin deep.

"Just be nice to Daisy, okay?" DJ frowned. "Don't hurt her feelings."

"Well, I don't know how I could be any nicer." Eliza spun around. "A free makeover, fashion advice, and the chance to model in New York. How much nicer can a person get?"

"I mean, be nice as in not tearing her down," DJ lowered her voice as she heard the toilet flush and the sink faucet running. "She already has low self-esteem. I don't want to see her beat up." DJ glanced over to where Kriti was quietly watching them with a fashion magazine open in her lap.

"Don't worry about Miss Daisy. She's in good hands now." Eliza winked as Daisy emerged from the bathroom.

"So ..." said Eliza as Daisy cautiously entered the room. "Let's see, where to begin here."

Daisy looked very uneasy now—kind of like a deer in the headlights. DJ just hoped she didn't make a run for it.

"Well, you *are* tall," said Eliza as she had Daisy turn around for her. "And you're thin too."

"So I've heard." Just then Daisy tripped over the area rug by the bed. DJ caught her by the hand and helped her regain her balance.

"But you might need walking lessons," said Eliza a bit snidely.

"I promised Daisy that you'd be *helpful*, Eliza."

"Of course, I'll be helpful." Eliza smirked at DJ. "But I'll also be honest." Eliza was standing in front of Daisy now. Because Daisy was about three inches taller than Eliza, she had to tilt her head up to peer closely at Daisy's face. "Can you handle honesty?"

"If it's meant to be constructive." Daisy frowned. "But if you're just ripping on me, I'll probably say adios, amiga."

"I *want* to help you." Eliza gave her a catty smile.

Just then someone knocked on the door. DJ opened it to let Rhiannon in. "Casey said you needed me."

"Yes," said Eliza. "It's time for Project Daisy."

"Project?" Daisy looked even more concerned now.

"Sorry," said DJ quickly. "Eliza didn't mean it like that."

"Yes ... yes ..." Eliza nodded to Rhiannon now. "Grab that pad and pencil over there, okay? You can take notes for me."

Rhiannon got the items, then sat down on the window seat and waited. "I'm ready when you are."

"Okay ..." Eliza pressed her lips together and slowly walked around Daisy, looking up and down as if taking a full inventory. "Obviously, the hair is all wrong. And it's so damaged that I think all we can do is cut it." She turned to Kriti. "Is that the January *Vogue*? Look for the Ralph Lauren ad. You know, the girl in the peacoat standing on a dock?"

Kriti flipped through the magazine until she finally located it. "This one?"

"Yeah. See her hair?"

"Cute," said Daisy.

Eliza ripped out the ad and shoved it at Rhiannon. "We'll send this with her to the salon. Same cut. Same highlights. It'll be perfect." Next, Eliza took Daisy to the bathroom where she and Rhiannon gave her a quick facial. They brought her back into the bedroom to begin applying makeup. DJ had discovered an unsolved Sudoku puzzle in the back of a magazine and was attempting to work it, casually listening as the girls experimented with the makeup on Daisy. She really wanted to sneak out, but suspected that Eliza would get mad since this was supposed to be a "group project."

"How's that?" Eliza pushed Daisy in front of DJ, waiting as if for approval.

DJ blinked in surprise. "Wow, she looks really good, Eliza. Nice job." Okay, it wasn't easy to admit that maybe Eliza really did know what she was doing.

"Thank you." Eliza nodded in satisfaction.

Now Daisy peered at herself in the closet door mirror and smiled. "Hey, I do look better. Cool."

"This is just the beginning," said Eliza. "We'll try to get you in for a cut tomorrow after school. Then we'll do some quick clothes shopping—just one outfit for now. We'll figure out the rest later. Is that okay, Daisy?"

"Sure, I guess."

"We'll start the complete makeover on Friday night and finish it on Saturday morning. DJ will present you to her grandmother at breakfast."

"Me?" DJ wasn't too sure about this.

"Yes, you. She's your grandmother, DJ."

"But you're the best sweet-talker," pointed out DJ.

"You do the introduction, and I'll jump in and back you up," promised Eliza. Then she turned back to Daisy. "Plan on spending the night here on Friday. Okay?"

"You're willing to give up your Friday night for me?"

"It's an investment in our future," said Eliza in a business tone. "We want Fashion Week to be a success."

"And fun," added Kriti.

"But if Madison and Tina go, that will not be the case," said DJ.

"So, are you in?" Eliza asked Daisy.

"I guess so."

"It won't be easy," warned Eliza. "You have to be willing to work hard."

Daisy nodded slowly. "I'm willing."

"Meet me after school tomorrow," commanded Eliza.

"But I have basketball practice."

"Make an excuse," said Eliza.

"Friday is a short practice anyway," DJ reminded her. "You probably won't be missed."

"You're sure?"

"I'll make an excuse for you," DJ assured her.

"Good," said Eliza. "Now meet me by the east exit," she told Daisy. "Do not be late. Do you understand?"

Daisy saluted her. "Yes, ma'am."

Eliza barely laughed. "You may think I'm kidding, but you have just enlisted in Eliza's boot camp. Don't expect this to be a walk in the park."

As DJ drove Daisy home, she was about to apologize for Eliza when Daisy spoke up. "This is going to be so awesome, DJ."

"Really? You're up for it?"

"I can't wait."

"Wow ... cool."

Daisy sighed happily. "This is like a dream come true for me."

"Seriously?" Now DJ couldn't even wrap her head around this. Eliza's makeover madness sounded like pure torture to her. And she should know since she'd been through pretty much the same thing herself. In fact, thanks to her grandmother, DJ felt like she was stuck in permanent makeover mode, like it would never end. But Daisy seemed to be welcoming it.

"Yes. I can't wait to see how it turns out, DJ. I mean, I know that I'm plain and homely and gawky and—"

"You're not—"

"Don't try to be nice, DJ. I know what I look like. I have mirrors in my house. I've heard other girls making fun of me enough times."

"Girls can be so brutal. And some of them put way too much importance on superficial things like appearances. Trust me, Daisy, I know. But, really, it's what's inside that counts, right?"

"Maybe ... but I've always had this dream ... you know, this great hope that someday ... somehow I'd grow up to be a beautiful swan—remember that story 'The Ugly Duckling'?"

"Yeah."

"Well, I always related to that ugly duckling. Big and clumsy, never fitting in. I've dreamed of waking up someday and finding I was pretty. I've wished and even prayed for it. But it just never seemed like anything other than a fantasy, you know?"

"Until now ..." Of course, even as DJ said this, she wasn't so sure that Daisy's dream was going to come true. For all DJ knew, it could turn into a nightmare. Oh, sure, Eliza claimed to know all there was to know about fashion and beauty, but what if Daisy proved to be too much of a challenge for her? What if Eliza's makeover didn't work? What if Grandmother rejected Daisy? Or, even worse, what if Grandmother said something mean to her?

"Oh, man ... if I could look even one-fourth as beautiful as Eliza ... or you, DJ, I'd be deliriously happy."

"I'm *not* beautiful."

"You are too!"

"Well, you know what they say ... beauty's in the eye of the beholder."

"Take it from me, you're beautiful. All you Carter House girls are beautiful. Everyone says so. Oh, they might be jealous of you guys, but I've heard them talking. They know you're all beautiful."

"Thanks." DJ cleared her throat. "And I'm sure you will be too ... when Eliza's done with you. But don't forget, she's only working on the surface. Like I said, you're beautiful on the inside, Daisy, and that's what really matters."

"That's easy for you to say. But I'd like to be pretty on the outside too."

"Don't worry." But even as she said this, she had her doubts. More than that, DJ wondered if she was compromising her

107

own values by participating in Eliza's beautification project. Since when had she cared about things like this? If she could do as she liked, she would simply go her way and let Grandmother and girls like Eliza go theirs. As it was, it seemed that not only did their paths continuously cross, they became so entangled that sometimes it was hard to tell them apart.

Daisy let out another happy sigh as DJ pulled into her driveway. "It's just too good to be true," she said dreamily. She opened the car door, then turned back to DJ. "I can't believe you picked me for this, DJ. You're such a good friend! See ya tomorrow."

"See ya," DJ called back. But as she drove away, she replayed Daisy's words . . . *too good to be true*. Daisy was probably right. It *was* too good to be true. Oh, what if they were simply setting poor Daisy up to fall on her face? What if she was in for a huge disappointment? That would be too cruel. Why had DJ allowed herself to be pulled in?

As DJ drove home, she prayed for Daisy. Not that she would miraculously wake up and be beautiful by Saturday. But that she wouldn't get hurt in the process. If worse came to worst, that DJ would be prepared to pick up the pieces. Chances are there would be pieces.

10

New York Debut

BY FRIDAY NIGHT, IT SEEMED that Project Daisy, as Eliza insisted upon calling it, had become top secret. Not only that, but Eliza had taken complete control. While somewhat relieved that she wasn't expected to help, DJ wasn't sure if this was such a good thing. But since she didn't hear any screaming coming from Eliza's room—and she knew that Daisy could probably take Eliza—she wasn't terribly worried. She *was* curious, and she was concerned that Daisy might be overly influenced by Eliza—or deeply hurt.

Kriti told DJ that Eliza had taken Daisy to her hair salon, as planned, and then sneaked her up to her room without anyone besides Kriti seeing her.

"I couldn't even see her hair since she had a hat on."

"But did Daisy seem okay?" asked DJ.

"I guess. Or else she was in complete shock." Kriti put her hand over her mouth and giggled. "As you know, Eliza is a force to be reckoned with."

"I know." DJ frowned. "That's what worries me."

"But I think Daisy is all right," Kriti reassured her.

But Eliza and Daisy didn't come down for dinner that evening. According to Clara, they were eating their dinner in Eliza's room. Not that it would've mattered if they'd joined them since Grandmother had gone out.

"Eliza is really taking this thing seriously," said Casey as she poured dressing onto her salad. "I asked for a sneak peek, and Eliza said to forget it."

"But we're supposed to be in on this too," said Rhiannon. "It's not fair for her to shut us out."

"I'm kind of glad to be shut out," admitted DJ. "As long as she's being kind to Daisy."

"Well, I heard Daisy laughing before I came down just now," said Rhiannon.

"That's right," said Casey, "laughing so loud she was snorting like a bull horn."

"I wonder how Eliza will break her of that habit," mused DJ.

"Don't worry," said Kriti. "I'm sure she'll do it."

After dinner, DJ was still a little concerned about Daisy. Why was Eliza being so mysterious? So to be sure all was well, DJ knocked on Eliza's door. "Everything going okay in there?"

"We're fine," called Eliza.

"Do we get to see your progress?" asked Rhiannon hopefully.

"I already told you guys ..." Eliza's voice sounded slightly irritated. "The big reveal will be in the morning."

"Maybe Daisy needs a break," called out Casey.

"I'm all right," Daisy called back.

"You'll see her tomorrow." Eliza stuck her head out the door. "And don't forget, DJ, you need to ask your grandmother to allow Daisy to join in the sessions. Then I'll jump in, okay?"

"Okay."

"And we can be supportive of the idea too," said Rhiannon.

"Yeah," agreed Casey. "Daisy is my friend too."

"Thanks, you guys," called Daisy from somewhere in the room.

So it seemed that all was under control. And if Eliza got Daisy to look halfway good, and if they all gently pressured Grandmother, DJ had no doubts that she'd let Daisy in. The big question was would Daisy have what it took to make it to New York? DJ imagined Daisy tripping over her own feet on the catwalk and what Grandmother might say. Still, it seemed worth the chance. Especially considering what she'd over-heard Madison say to Tina in the lunch line earlier today. Naturally, the girls didn't know that DJ, who just happened to be standing behind a post, had also been listening.

"I have it all figured out," Madison had quietly told Tina. "With Taylor Mitchell off at rehab, we should get in for sure. My mom saw Mrs. Carter at the Chic Boutique yesterday, and she said that Mrs. Carter told her that she was going to pick the taller girls."

"Fashion Week, here we come," said Tina.

Just then, the line had moved forward, and DJ had moved out from behind the post. Naturally the two girls pretended not to see DJ—or acted like they didn't care. Just then Conner had come up. So DJ began talking to him—a good thing since she'd been tempted to inform those catty girls not to hold their breath since Taylor *was* coming home. But that would've blown Taylor's plan for surprising everyone.

Even so, she did tell Eliza and the others about Madison and Tina's confidence that they were going to New York. Eliza had assured them of her foolproof plan, which included special "tutoring sessions" to ensure that Ariel and Haley would both be chosen. "And, if necessary, I have some other plans to make sure that no one else has a chance."

"You're not going to do anything mean, are you?" Rhiannon had asked with concern.

"Of course not." Eliza had given her most innocent look.

Still, DJ wasn't convinced. She knew what Eliza was capable of when she was determined to get her way.

"So Haley, Ariel, Daisy, plus the five of us makes eight." Eliza had smiled like she'd just completed a complicated algebraic equation.

Of course, as DJ was trying to go to sleep that night, she realized there was a flaw in Eliza's math — she had left Taylor out of the equation. Naturally, Eliza assumed that Taylor wouldn't make it back from rehab in time to do Fashion Week. DJ was pretty sure Eliza didn't want Taylor to come back in time. And now Eliza was getting those three girls' hopes up.

But once Taylor came home, one of those girls would be in for a big disappointment. DJ suspected it would be Daisy. And that made her feel guilty. Why had she gotten involved in Eliza's little games? Seriously, why did she even care? Except that she didn't want to see Daisy hurt. She didn't want her "Ugly Duckling" story to wind up with a sad ending.

The following morning, when Eliza invited DJ to come to her room for a sneak preview, DJ suddenly realized her worries were for nothing.

"Wow," she said to both Eliza and Daisy. "This is amazing."

"I know," agreed Daisy as she stared at herself in the mirror. "I feel like I'm dreaming. I keep pinching myself."

Eliza shook her finger at her. "And I keep telling her to stop that or she'll end up with ugly bruises on her arms."

112

"You look fantastic, Daisy!" DJ honestly could not believe her eyes. "If I saw you on the street, I wouldn't know it was you." She turned to Eliza. "You are *really* good at this."

Eliza beamed with pride. "Why, thank you!"

Daisy's previously mousy brown hair now had shining golden highlights and was cut into spiky layers that framed her face and softened her features. The cut of her hair and the highlights made her brown eyes look big and sparkly. And the makeup and concealer were so well done that DJ couldn't spot a single zit. And Daisy's outfit, while not over the top, was attractively sophisticated with slim, tapered black pants topped with a pale blue sweater. DJ suspected the cashmere sweater belonged to Eliza since she recalled Grandmother complimenting her on it before. Also, pale blue was Grandmother's favorite color.

"Very nice," said DJ. She turned back to Eliza again. "Really, well done."

"Now, walk," Eliza commanded.

Daisy slowly walked back and forth across the bedroom, executing a nearly perfect turn. "How's that?"

"Still needs work," said Eliza. "But it's better." She turned to DJ. "I'll keep her in flats until she gets better at it. Besides, she's certainly tall enough for flats."

"Wait until Grandmother meets her."

"That's why I gave you a sneak preview," said Eliza. "I have a revised plan."

Eliza's plan was to be nonchalant. Daisy just happened to be a friend from school who'd stopped by. "Let your grandmother be the one to invite her in," finished Eliza.

DJ nodded. Eliza was absolutely right. Daisy couldn't help but catch Grandmother's eye, and Grandmother couldn't possibly resist this tall, thin, pretty girl. "Great idea."

"So you bring Daisy down a few minutes late," continued Eliza. "Casually introduce her and then leave it to me to lead the conversation."

"Sounds good to me."

It was hard to admit it, but Eliza had both brains and beauty. If she could only be a little bit kinder beneath that flawless exterior. Or at least a little more genuine.

"Are you nervous?" DJ asked Daisy as they slowly made their way downstairs.

"It's weird," Daisy said quietly. "But I feel incredibly calm. It's like I'm someone else now. Does that make sense?"

"As long as you don't change underneath it all." DJ turned to glance at the tall, elegant beauty walking beside her. "I liked who you were already, Daisy."

"Thank you." But even the way Daisy said this sounded a bit different from before. In fact, it sounded somewhat like Eliza. Hopefully Eliza wasn't simply cloning Daisy into another one of herself.

"You're late, Desiree," began Grandmother.

"My apologies," said DJ. "But my friend Daisy dropped in." Then DJ politely introduced Daisy to Grandmother and the others. "I invited her to stay for breakfast."

"A pleasure to meet you, dear." Grandmother picked up the silver bell by her plate and rang it. "Set another place, please, Clara."

"Daisy is on the basketball team with Casey and me," said DJ as she spread a napkin in her lap.

"I'm surprised that Daisy didn't sign up for your Saturday sessions, Mrs. Carter," said Eliza innocently.

Grandmother looked slightly perplexed. "Perhaps Daisy was unaware of what we're doing here at Carter House."

114

She looked directly at DJ now. "Did you tell Daisy about our classes?"

DJ shrugged. "I didn't think she'd be interested."

"What kind of classes?" asked Daisy, just as smoothly as Eliza might've done.

"Modeling sessions," explained Rhiannon. "We're going to model in New York, for Fashion Week."

"Oh, that sounds exciting." Daisy turned and smiled brightly at Grandmother.

"Exciting?" Grandmother's eyes lit up. "Are you interested in modeling?"

Daisy looked down ever so slightly, the same way Eliza would do if she were playing coy. "Oh, I doubt that anyone would be interested in me, but it does sound like fun."

Grandmother cleared her throat. "Perhaps you're not aware that I've been quite involved in the fashion industry, Daisy. And I can safely say that you seem to have what it takes to make a fine model."

"Really?" Daisy acted surprised.

"Of course, one never knows until one gives it a try."

Daisy nodded. "Of course."

"But if you're truly interested, why don't you stay for the session and see how you like it — *for free*."

"Oh, thank you," gushed Daisy. "That would be great."

Grandmother nodded as if extremely pleased with herself. DJ almost laughed to see that Eliza made the exact same gesture. Maybe they really were cut of the same cloth. Anyway, Eliza's plan had worked, and it was clear that she was feeling good. And when they went to the third floor for their session, Eliza kept Daisy close to her. It was obvious that Project Daisy was still in progress as Eliza quietly coached her and Daisy obediently listened. She was obviously enjoying Eliza's attention. But that wasn't the only attention she was getting.

As soon as the other girls arrived, it was clear that all eyes were on "the new girl." No one even recognized her. And when DJ introduced the new mystery model, suppressing the urge to chuckle, they couldn't believe it was really Daisy Kempton. Then, as the Carter House girls sat together with Daisy, Haley, and Ariel, it became rather apparent that alliances were forming, lines were being drawn. And both Madison and Tina looked seriously irritated. It was obvious they were being shut out, and they were not a bit happy.

DJ had taken care with her appearance this morning. No way did she want to be her grandmother's bad example again today. Today's focus was skin care and makeup. And while DJ wasn't nearly as polished as Eliza and Taylor, she had learned a thing or two the past several months. She was greatly relieved when Grandmother selected Madison to point out "some common mistakes that young girls make when applying makeup." DJ was surprised to feel a twinge of pity for Madison as she stood in front of the group, receiving Grandmother's overly frank critique of her cosmetics.

"The lips are too harsh," said Grandmother. "That's due to the lip liner, which should always be used sparingly. But besides that, the color is all wrong. She's picked a warm shade when she obviously needs a cool one. Also, you girls need to decide what part of your face you wish to accentuate. Naturally, you should pick your best feature—either your eyes or your lips. Not both." Grandmother peered at Madison. "In Madison's case, I'm not sure which that would be. But it's clear that poor Madison couldn't make up her mind either. Consequently, she overdid it on both her eyes and her lips. And she ends up looking clownish or like a lady of the night."

Grandmother droned on at Madison's expense, and although DJ felt sorry for her, she had to agree that both Madison and Tina tended to overdo the makeup. Perhaps they really were learning a thing or two from Grandmother. Or maybe they would figure out that their chances of going to New York were rapidly diminishing and simply drop out of the sessions altogether. That would make it so much easier for everyone.

After the session ended and Grandmother had made her exit, Eliza offered some extra tutoring help to Haley, Ariel, and Daisy. "That is if you want to stick around after school," she joked. Of course, they all eagerly accepted.

"First, we'll practice the catwalk," she was explaining when Madison and Tina marched over and confronted her.

"Why only them?" demanded Madison.

"Why not?" Eliza stood straighter and eyed them coolly.

"Because it's *not* fair," said Tina.

"Not fair?" Eliza gave them a puzzled look now. "What are you talking about?"

"You can't give them special coaching and leave the rest of us out of it."

"I can if I like," said Eliza.

"I'm telling Mrs. Carter," said Tina.

Eliza just laughed. "Go ahead. For your information, what I do with my time is up to me. Mrs. Carter will probably be happy to hear that I'm volunteering to coach a few girls."

"Why not coach anyone who wants it?" asked Madison a bit more softly.

"Because I don't want to."

"How about you then?" Tina turned to DJ and Casey, who were standing by and watching with interest.

"Me?" DJ actually laughed. "You'd have to be pretty desperate to ask me for help. Everyone here knows that I'm the klutz in the group."

"That's true," said Madison sharply.

"What about Casey then?" asked Tina.

"Hey, you're the ones who were bragging about going to New York," taunted Casey. "I wouldn't think you'd need any special help."

"But maybe you *should* talk to my grandmother," said DJ. She saw the sparks in Madison's eyes and wanted to defuse the situation.

"Fine," snapped Madison. "If this is how it's going to be, I'm going to ask Mrs. Carter for a full refund."

DJ just shrugged. "Hey, it's a free country. You can ask her if you want." But as the disgruntled girls made their exit, DJ couldn't help but giggle as she tried to envision her grandmother handing them back their tuition. "Good luck with that."

"Yeah," said Casey.

Of course, what they didn't know then, and what they found out later, was that Grandmother had been so "touched" by the girls' strong interest in modeling that she'd given Madison and Tina an old VHS tape from Fashion Week, taken about a decade ago. But she encouraged them to go home and study the tape and practice during their free time.

11

New York Debut

"GET A LOAD OF MADISON AND TINA." Casey nodded toward the cafeteria entrance as she and DJ set their food trays at their favorite table.

DJ looked up in time to see Madison and Tina striding into the room like they thought they were on the catwalk with all eyes on them. They were dressed like they'd exchanged high school for nine-to-five jobs in a Manhattan high-rise. Watching the two girls sauntering through the cafeteria, DJ could almost hear her grandmother's voice directing each move. *Shoulders back, hips forward, elongated strides, one foot directly ahead of the next.* Had they downloaded Grandmother's words into their iPods?

"That is so over the top." DJ couldn't help but giggle.

"They're like the Stepford models." Casey snickered. "Brainwashed by Mrs. Carter."

Suddenly they were both laughing loudly. But when Madison and Tina drew closer and glanced at their table, DJ stifled her giggles. She suddenly looked down at her food tray, pretending to be highly amused by her soda straw as she peeled off the paper and stuck it into her Sierra Mist.

"If looks could kill," said Casey quietly, "we'd be history."

"What's with Madison and Tina?" asked Kriti as she and Eliza joined them at the table.

"It looked like they were practicing the hostile-yet-bored expression," said Eliza. "With an emphasis on the hostile." Then she did a perfect imitation of their faces, causing the whole table to erupt into laughter.

"What's so funny?" asked Rhiannon as she joined them.

"Madison and Tina," whispered Casey.

"They do seem to be taking their modeling training a bit seriously," admitted Rhiannon as she peered over to where the girls were standing—rather posing—in the lunch line now. "Look at the height of those heels," she pointed out. "Their feet are going to be killing them by the end of the day."

"I think they want to look taller," said Kriti.

"Like it matters." DJ shook her head. "Seriously, who's looking? Who cares?"

"We're looking." Casey chuckled.

"Well, don't," commanded Eliza. "Let's not give them the satisfaction."

"Hello," said Harry as he took the seat next to Eliza. "Mind if I join you pretty ladies?"

"As long as you keep the compliments flowing," said Eliza coyly.

Harry's eyes suddenly grew wide as he stared at the cafeteria entrance. "Who *is* that?"

They all looked over to see Daisy walking in. Dressed in a short pink skirt—that DJ thought had once belonged to Eliza—and a cute little denim jacket, Daisy made her way toward them. With her shoulders squared and head held high, she seemed to be focusing on each step, like she was afraid she was going to trip and fall. Then, just a few feet away from their table, she looked uncertainly at Eliza.

"That's the new Daisy Kempton," said DJ quietly.

"Eliza's project," added Casey.

"Come on over." Eliza waved at Daisy.

Daisy smiled and approached.

"Have a seat," offered DJ.

"Thank you." Daisy sat down and removed a small brown sack from her oversized D&G bag. That too looked familiar, probably another one of Eliza's castoffs.

"How's your day going?" DJ said to Daisy.

"It's *so* weird."

"What's that?" asked Casey.

"No one even knows who I am." Daisy giggled self-consciously. "It's like they think I'm a *new* student. Even my teachers don't get it. Mr. Myers actually marked me absent in social studies, and he made me show him my ID to prove it was really me. So weird."

"But is that okay with you?" asked DJ.

Daisy smiled now. "Oh, yeah, totally."

Although Daisy seemed happy enough, DJ felt concerned for her. How would she deal with all this attention? It was obvious the guys were looking her way now. In fact, Taylor's main guy, Seth, couldn't keep his eyes off of Daisy during lunch. Oh, he didn't say anything, but DJ suspected that if Taylor didn't get back soon, Seth might ask Daisy out. How would Taylor feel to be dumped by Seth for someone like Daisy Kempton? Not that DJ would mind if Taylor and Seth broke up. Especially now that Taylor had done rehab. Seriously, Seth could be bad news for Taylor. On the other hand, he could be bad news for Daisy too.

"Earth to DJ," said Conner quietly.

121

"Huh?" DJ turned to him and smiled. "Was I spacing?"

"Yeah, a little."

"Sorry."

"Are you done?"

She looked at her tray and grinned. "Looks like it."

"Want me to walk you to class?"

"Sure."

Once they'd dumped their trays and were away from the others, DJ admitted her concerns for Daisy. "I'm just worried she won't be able to handle it. I mean, at first I was worried that I was setting her up for a disappointment," she told him. "That we'd get her hopes up for going to New York and then she'd be let down. But now I'm pretty sure that my grandmother will pick her to model."

"She sure looks like a model." Conner shook his head. "I didn't even recognize her."

"You're not the only one," said DJ. "Seth looked like he wanted to have her for dessert."

Conner laughed. "It is kind of a shocking transformation."

"Well, she might be a head-turner now, but Daisy is a sweet girl underneath all that glam, and this kind of attention could mess with her mind."

"How so?"

"Oh, I don't know. I guess I'm just tired of all this." DJ sighed.

"All this what?"

"All this obsessive focus on appearances. It's like my grandmother is spreading her beauty poison everywhere. First it infects Carter House. Now it's all over Crescent Cove High. It's like superficiality is contagious—epidemic even. And the truth is I just get sick and tired of it!"

"Now, tell me how you really feel."

She looked at him and laughed. "Sorry. I guess I just needed to vent."

"That's okay. But you know what's really cool?"

"What?"

"All that focus on fashion and beauty don't seem to change you, DJ."

Suddenly she felt slightly defensive. "Is that your way of saying that I'm not fashionable or beautiful?"

He laughed. "No way. That's not what I'm saying. You are definitely fashionable and beautiful." He lowered his voice now. "But you do it naturally. It's just who you are, DJ. It's like you don't even have to try."

She chuckled. "Well, my grandmother wouldn't agree with that. But thank you just the same."

"It doesn't turn your head either. You just go on being who you are — your real self. You do sports, and you have a good time, and it just doesn't obsess you." He discreetly nodded over to where Tina and Madison were striding along the other side of the breezeway now. "Not the way it does some people."

"Okay, I'll take that as a compliment."

Still, DJ felt aggravated by the end of the day. She couldn't wait until their New York debut was over and everyone could get back to life as normal. Not that she really knew what normal was. But all this fashion nonsense made her feel weary.

Things didn't seem to improve much as the week wore on. Madison and Tina continued to strut their stuff at school, acting as if every day was just one more dress rehearsal for Fashion Week. Eliza continued tutoring Daisy, Haley, and Ariel as well as making her superior comments and observations about others. DJ caught Kriti throwing away her untouched lunch. And Rhiannon thought she was getting an ulcer.

"An ulcer?" asked DJ as they walked to geometry together.

"I've been having stomachaches," Rhiannon confessed. "And I think it might be stress related."

"Seriously?"

She shrugged. "Maybe."

"But you always seem so laid-back and well-adjusted, Rhiannon. I don't get it."

"I try to be laid-back. And I've been praying that God will give me strength. But sometimes I feel like I'm living in a 24/7 beauty pageant. I mean, day and night it's all that Eliza talks about. It's all your grandmother talks about. And now Haley is asking me to help her to prepare for New York. And I want to be nice, but at the same time, I want to say forget it."

"So, why don't you?"

"Because I want to be nice."

"You need to be nice to yourself too," said DJ. "I mean, isn't it okay to live your own life, to focus on what you enjoy, what you're good at? Like your art and designing and stuff."

"I guess so. But all this modeling business feels like it's taking over."

"Only if we let it."

"Yeah . . . you're right."

"And, really, Rhiannon. You're the sweetest person I know. But it's not like you have to take care of everyone. That would give anyone an ulcer."

"Maybe . . ."

"So why not just give yourself a break. Remember last week's sermon about loving others as we love ourselves?"

Rhiannon nodded.

"So, don't forget to love yourself."

She smiled now. "Thanks for the sermon, DJ."

"Was I preaching at you?"

Rhiannon laughed. "A little. But I liked it. And I needed it."

"I'll be glad when Fashion Week is just a memory."

"Me too. Although I am looking forward to visiting the design studios."

"I'm so thankful we decided to do basketball this season." DJ mopped her brow with a sweat towel as she and Casey and Daisy exited the gym on Thursday afternoon.

"You mean because we won today?" Casey asked as she pushed open the locker-room door.

"No. I mean because it's one part of my life that has nothing to do with fashion."

Casey chuckled as she tugged at DJ's sweat-soaked shirt. "Are you saying these foxy uniforms aren't styling?"

"They're stylish enough for me."

"Me too," agreed Casey. "I'm counting the days until Fashion Week is over and done with."

"You and me both," said DJ as she opened her locker. "I'm sick of fashion."

"You mean you don't like fashion?" Daisy looked incredulous.

"Not particularly." DJ peeled of her wet shirt and tossed it to the floor.

"But you're a Carter House girl," said Daisy.

DJ just laughed. "Please, *don't* remind me."

Daisy just shook her head. "Man, I wish we could trade places."

As she peeled off her shorts, DJ considered this. If it were even a distinct possibility, she might've taken Daisy up on the offer. But, although Grandmother approved of Daisy, she probably wouldn't approve of a switch.

"Do either of you have any conditioner?" asked Daisy as she wrapped a towel around like a sarong. "Eliza said I need to take care of—"

"Here you go," said DJ as she thrust a bottle at her. "This is really good stuff. Taylor made me start using it when I was swimming."

Soon they were all in the showers, laughing and joking as they showered and shampooed.

"You're not washing your hair, DJ?" asked Casey as she borrowed DJ's conditioner from Daisy.

"No. I'm going out with Conner as soon as I'm done here. By the way, that means you can drive my car home . . . if you don't mind."

Casey grinned as she rubbed conditioner into her short hair. "No problem as far as—" Suddenly she stopped and pointed across the shower room. "What the—?"

"Huh?" DJ turned to see Daisy bent over and rinsing her hair now—her *blue* hair! "Daisy Kempton, what is wrong with your hair?" she shouted.

Daisy stood up straight with a confused expression. "What?" But not only was her hair blue, her face and hands were blue too.

"Look at your hands!" shrieked another girl.

"What?" Daisy stared at her blue hands, then her eyes grew really huge. "Look at Casey!" she shrieked.

DJ turned around to see that Casey's hair, like Daisy's, was turning blue. Not the exact same shade, more of a purplish blue, but definitely blue. "Rinse your hair!" yelled DJ. "Hurry!"

Casey looked down at her own hands now and immediately began to rinse off. "What is going on?" she sputtered as she rubbed and rinsed her hair.

126

While other girls laughed and teased Casey and Daisy, DJ went over and took her bottle of conditioner off the shower shelf and examined it.

"It's not coming off," screamed Casey as she looked at her blue hands.

"What did you do to that conditioner?" cried Daisy from across the room where she was standing in front of the steamed-up mirror and staring at her blue image in horror.

"Hey, maybe you two can join the Blue Man Group," suggested Tawnee. "Take it to Vegas."

Of course, everyone laughed. Everyone except Daisy and Casey. And despite her efforts at self-control, DJ snickered.

"Did you sabotage us?" demanded Casey as the three of them stood in front of the foggy mirror.

DJ was still holding the bottle of conditioner. "Of course not!"

"Well, it's pretty convenient that you didn't wash *your* hair, DJ." Casey turned and gave DJ a very accusatory look.

"What are you saying?"

"I'm saying that you go and loan both of us your conditioner and we look like this!"

"You're the one who asked to use it," DJ reminded her.

Now Daisy was actually crying. "I knew something would happen to make my dream end," she sobbed. "I knew that it couldn't last."

Casey turned to face DJ, holding her blue hair in her blue hands and looking angry. "You better explain what's going on here!"

"Hey, you used to like blue hair," DJ said lightly.

"Desiree Jeannette Lane!" Casey shook her fist in the air now. "Tell us what is going on!"

Suddenly DJ remembered something. "Hey, when we came in from the game ... my lock was open on my locker ... it was in place, but it was unlocked. I thought I must've left it open."

"You think someone got into your locker?" asked Casey.

DJ ran over to her locker and picked up the lock to see if it looked like it had been broken, but it seemed fine. So she closed it shut and it locked just fine too. But when she tried her combination, slowly turning 12–22–34, it didn't work. She tried it again. "Hey, you guys, this isn't even my lock!"

Now Daisy and Casey were over by the lockers, looking at the lock too.

"You know ... I saw Tina and Madison out in the hallway by the locker room after school," said Daisy. "Do you think—"

"These locks aren't hard to break," said Casey. "I'm sure a crowbar could easily pop one open."

DJ held up the conditioner. "And then someone could slip something into my conditioner ... and put another lock on my locker to keep me from being suspicious."

"Maybe so ...." Casey frowned. "And Madison used to have PE the same period as we did. She might've remembered where your locker was."

"Still, it's hard to imagine Madison running around with a crowbar in her purse."

"It seems a little farfetched," agreed Daisy.

DJ looked at Casey and Daisy and had to control herself from laughing at their wildly colored hair, which was bad enough, but their blue-tinted faces were even worse. "I'm really sorry about this mess, you guys," she told them. "I mean, if I had any idea that someone had tampered with this ..." She held up the bottle and shook her head. "I never—"

"I know," said Casey. "This whole thing has Madison and Tina written all over it."

"Too bad their fingerprints aren't on it too," said DJ.

"I'm telling Ms. Jones," proclaimed Daisy as she wrapped her towel more tightly around herself. "Those girls need to be punished."

"What kind of dye do you think they used in here?" DJ set the despicable bottle down on the bench and began to get dressed.

"I don't know, but my guess is that it's fairly permanent," growled Casey. She was flinging on her clothes now. "I refuse to take this lying down. I intend to do something about it!"

"Ms. Jones wants to talk to all of us," Daisy informed them.

So in various stages of dress, they all went to her office and told their versions of the weird story.

"It just had to be Madison and Tina," declared Casey angrily. But when Ms. Jones questioned about how they knew this for certain, no one could really say anything to prove it.

"Here's a website with suggestions for how to get rid of dye," Ms. Jones said as she pointed to her laptop screen. "It says that dye can last up to three days on skin. But there are a few things you can do like exfoliating and using special creams to remove it." She wrote down the name of the website and handed it to Casey.

"That's helpful, but what about Madison and Tina?" demanded Casey. "Shouldn't they get in trouble for this?"

"There's not much you can do unless you have evidence. Do you think anyone witnessed them tampering with DJ's locker?"

"I'll ask around," said DJ.

"I've taken your statements. Naturally, if I find anything out, I'll be happy to do something about it. But without evidence ..." Ms. Jones held up her hands hopelessly. "In the meantime, I'll hang onto that conditioner and the lock ... in case we can use it as evidence."

DJ handed over the bottle and lock. "This is so wrong."

Now Ms. Jones studied DJ. "So, DJ, how did you get off without turning blue too?"

"DJ has a big date tonight," said Casey in a snippy tone. "She didn't want to go out with wet hair."

"Which reminds me, I better get going." DJ looked sympathetically at her two blue friends. "Really, you guys, I'm so sorry this happened." Then DJ hurried to finish dressing and went out to find Conner waiting near the gym. She quickly relayed the incident to him, and he ended up laughing so hard that she wanted to punch him. "It's not that funny," she said for the umpteenth time.

"I know ... I know ..." He helped her into the truck. "All that for a fashion show? Man, I just don't get how girls can be so mean sometimes."

She leaned back into the seat and sighed. "When will the madness end?"

12

NEW YORK DEBUT

"I need to ask a favor," DJ told Conner after they had finished dinner and were leaving the restaurant.

"What's that?"

"Well, I know this was supposed to be a date, but the truth is I had an ulterior motive when I agreed to go out tonight."

"Huh?"

"Can you keep a secret?"

He chuckled. "Hey, this is starting to sound intriguing."

So she told Conner that Taylor had called the night before and had told DJ about her surprise arrival. "I thought it would be less suspicious if I appeared to be out with you when we picked her up at the airport."

"Taylor's at the airport?"

DJ glanced at her watch. "Not yet. But in about half an hour."

"Let's go," he said as he took her hand and jogged over to his pickup.

"Why doesn't she want anyone to know she's here?" he asked as he drove. "I thought Taylor enjoyed the limelight. You'd think she'd want a big splashy welcome home."

"She sort of does." So DJ explained Taylor's plan to surprise everyone at tomorrow's session.

"Man, it'd be fun to be a fly on the wall there. Girls with blue hair. Madison and Tina planning mean tricks. Taylor fresh out of rehab and ready to dethrone Queen Eliza."

DJ started to giggle. "Hey, maybe I tell you too much, Conner. You could probably do some blackmailing if you wanted to earn some cash."

"You can trust me." He laughed. "Still, I gotta hand it to you girls. You seem to have a lot more excitement than us guys."

"Excitement at a high price." Then she reminded him of Rhiannon's stomachaches, Kriti's eating disorder, and Taylor's stint in rehab. "It's not all fun and games."

Conner decided to drop DJ off to find Taylor while he circled the terminal. "Just call me when you're ready to be picked up."

DJ thanked him and hurried inside to the baggage claim area. Taylor had already called to say that her plane had landed and that she was waiting for her bags. DJ felt a little nervous as she pressed through the crowds of people clamoring around the slow-moving conveyor belt. Would Taylor be different? Would she be as excited to see her as DJ was to see her? Just then she spotted Taylor reaching for a bag. Without even thinking, DJ broke into a run, straight for Taylor.

"Welcome home!" DJ shouted as she threw her arms around her. Taylor hugged her too, but when she stepped back, DJ could tell something was different. Something had changed.

"Thanks. It's good to see you."

"Here, I'll take that," offered DJ. "You get your other bags."

"Thanks."

DJ studied Taylor as she went over to snag another bag. She was still as strikingly beautiful as ever—maybe even more

132

so. But something had changed. Taylor turned and smiled as she held up her bag and pointed to another one slowly making its way around. DJ sensed there was a new softness in Taylor's features or maybe it was her expression . . . almost like a vulnerability. And, although DJ was happy that Taylor had changed, it still made her uneasy. Because she knew there were reasons that someone like Taylor still needed to be tough—it was like a cloak of protection that she wore against girls like Eliza or Madison or Tina.

DJ phoned Conner, and before long they were piling Taylor's bags into the back of his pickup. "Welcome back," he told Taylor as he opened the passenger door for the two girls.

"Thanks," said Taylor as DJ climbed in and slid to the middle. "It's good to be back."

"Back on the *outside*," teased DJ.

"Yes, free at last . . . free at last." She kind of laughed. "Actually it wasn't that bad. I know I needed it."

"And you're really ready to be out?" asked DJ.

"As ready as I can be. And, hey, if I mess up, they told me that I'm welcome back anytime."

DJ frowned. "But you're not planning on messing up, are you?"

"No . . . of course not."

As Conner drove them away from the terminal, DJ told Taylor about the latest developments at Carter House, filling her in on Project Daisy, Madison and Tina hoping to be picked to go to New York, Eliza acting like the Carter House queen, and finally about the two blue girls.

Taylor laughed loudly, and for a moment DJ thought it was the old Taylor again. "That's too bad," she said quietly. "I wonder how you get rid of something like that."

"Ms. Jones was giving them some tips from a website."

"I can't wait to see everyone," said Taylor. "It feels like it's been so long."

"And tomorrow you make your big surprise entrance?" asked Conner.

"I told Conner he had to keep this under his hat," DJ said quickly. "Although I don't know why you're being so secretive, since everyone will know you're back by tomorrow anyway."

"Oh, I just thought it would be fun to be dramatic." Taylor sighed. "You know me, I like catching people off guard."

"That's sure true," said Conner.

"I mean, I know I've changed," admitted Taylor. "But not completely."

"I hope not," said DJ. "I liked you before."

"Even when I was being rude or drunk or—"

"Okay, I didn't like *everything* about you."

"Me either." Taylor sighed again.

"Are you tired?" asked DJ.

"It's been a long day."

"So how are you going to sneak into Carter House unseen?" asked Conner as they drove through town.

"I'm not staying there tonight."

"Did you get a hotel?"

"Even better," Taylor told them. "I got a room at the bed-and-breakfast right down the street from Carter House. I'll just walk on over."

"Very cool," said DJ. "The session starts at nine o'clock sharp. We meet on the third floor where Grandmother has a full-size catwalk to practice on."

"Sounds good."

"I can't wait to see their faces when you show up," said DJ. "Particularly Eliza's. I think she's certain that you're history and that she's running the show." DJ almost mentioned how Eliza was feeling pretty comfortable, acting like she was special because she was the only girl with a "private room." But then DJ realized she'd have to disclose that Taylor's things were in there now. And she wasn't sure if Taylor would be happy to hear that bit of news. It could wait until later.

"I had time to do a little shopping in Beverly Hills yesterday," said Taylor as they unloaded her bags in the dark drive in front of the B&B. "I've got a killer outfit that Eliza will be drooling over tomorrow."

"Good for you!"

This time Taylor hugged DJ first. "It's so great to see you again, DJ. Thanks ... you know, for everything."

DJ nodded and smiled. "Thanks for coming back. You have no idea how much I missed you."

"I sort of know." Now Taylor got her old impish grin. "But let's not get carried away, sweetie. Conner might get jealous."

He laughed, and then they all said good-night.

"Hey, thanks for letting me play a part in this little drama," said Conner as he helped DJ back into the pickup.

"Thank you."

"Taylor seems different, doesn't she?" He drove the short distance down the street to Carter House, then parked in front.

"You noticed it too?"

"Sure." Conner helped her out of the truck now.

"I just hope she hasn't changed completely." DJ felt his hand grasp hers as he walked her up to the front porch. "I mean, some changes are good—like I really hope she never drinks again."

"I think you've been a good influence on Taylor."

DJ laughed quietly. "I don't know about that."

"Well, I do." Conner smiled and leaned down to kiss her, but then he simply kissed her forehead, which was rather nice. "And you're a good influence on me too!"

DJ wondered about that as she slipped into the quiet house. She'd like to think that she'd been a good influence on someone or something, but mostly she wasn't too sure. It was hard enough trying to figure out her own life, without trying to figure out how to influence others. But at least she could pray. So she tiptoed to the library and sat down and prayed, one by one, for everyone in the house. And then she prayed for Taylor, asking God to help Taylor and give her what it would take to stick to her recovery program.

"WHAT ON EARTH HAPPENED TO YOU?" demanded Grandmother when Casey showed up at the breakfast table looking slightly blue around the edges. Rhiannon had helped Casey with a special ointment and some exfoliating cream that they'd begged from Eliza, and although the blueness had faded considerably, it was still obvious that something was wrong.

"Someone sabotaged me," declared Casey in an angry tone.

"That's right," said DJ quickly. "Someone put blue dye in my hair conditioner, and both Casey and Daisy used it."

Grandmother peered at DJ now. "But you didn't?"

DJ just shook her head.

"We think we know who did it and we—"

"Never mind about that," said Grandmother sharply. "How do you think you'll look by next Thursday when we go to New York?"

"I already made a hair appointment for both Casey and Daisy," said Eliza. "Rena assured me that she can fix their hair color."

"And their skin?" Grandmother directed this to Eliza as if she was expected to have all the answers.

"It's supposed to be normal in about three days," DJ told her.

"It already looks much better than it did last night," added Rhiannon.

"And we can always use extra makeup," pointed out Eliza.

Grandmother sighed in exasperation. "Well, I had planned to make an important announcement regarding Fashion Week. Now I'm not so sure."

"Oh, Mrs. Carter," Eliza gushed sweetly. "Now, don't you go and let Casey's little incident get you down. Everything is going to be just peachy. I'm sure both Casey and Daisy will look perfectly gorgeous by Thursday."

"Yes, I suppose you're right." Grandmother seemed somewhat placated. Looking around the table, she actually smiled. "I wanted all of my Carter House girls to hear it first."

DJ couldn't help but glance over to where Taylor used to sit — the place where she'd be sitting again before the day was over. It took all of DJ's self-control not to grin with happiness over this secret. Instead, she turned her full attention to her grandmother. As had been the case the previous Saturdays, Grandmother was dressed elegantly this morning. Today she wore a pale green silk pantsuit with an ivory blouse and pearl accessories. Not over the top, simply tasteful. Like Grandmother.

"I had planned to save my announcement until our fashion training session this morning, but then I thought you girls deserve to hear it first." She cleared her throat and sat up straighter. "I have made my final decision about which three girls will be accompanying us to New York next week."

The table got very quiet now.

"Naturally, you girls are all going. Even our blue girl, who will hopefully look more normal by then." Grandmother frowned slightly. "I only wish that Taylor had made it back in time."

DJ pressed her lips together and waited.

"My first choice is Ariel Buford." Grandmother smiled. "I'm a bit surprised myself, but Ariel really seems to want this, and she's got the walk down beautifully. And with all her improvements in hair and makeup, well, I'm just very pleased to let her know that she'll be joining us."

DJ wanted to add that those "improvements" were probably mostly thanks to Eliza and Rhiannon since they'd helped her with hair and makeup.

"My next choice is our newest student, Daisy Kempton. Goodness, with her height and those legs, Dylan should be very happy."

"But I thought you said he wanted real-looking young women," DJ reminded her, mostly for Kriti's sake.

Grandmother nodded. "Oh, yes, dear. He does. But this is a fashion show. We must have some long-legged beauties in our midst."

DJ tried not to roll her eyes.

"My third choice is Madison Dormont," continued Grandmother.

Casey dropped her fork, and Kriti let out a little gasp.

Grandmother looked around at their surprised faces. "Is something wrong, girls?"

Eliza spoke up. "It's just that we're rather shocked, Mrs. Carter."

"Shocked? I don't see why. Madison has worked very hard, and I think she deserves to go."

Eliza nodded slowly. "Maybe so ... but I'm not sure that you know that much about Madison. Not like we do."

"What are you saying?"

"For one thing, we're almost certain that Madison was responsible for this," said Casey as she held up her blue hands.

"That's right," said DJ.

"Do you have proof?" asked Grandmother.

"No, but—"

"Certainly you girls must know that people are innocent until proven guilty in this country."

Casey let out a low groan. "Yeah, right."

"That's not all, Mrs. Carter ..." Eliza smoothly intervened. "Haven't you been trying to teach us about being ladies, using good etiquette and deportment and such?"

"Well, certainly. That's been my goal."

"And I hate to say it, but Madison Dormont hasn't been the most wholesome influence, especially when it comes to ... morals."

DJ tried not to laugh. Who was Eliza to talk about morals? Not that she didn't know what Eliza was up to. But since it was Madison they were discussing, well, DJ wasn't going to jump to her defense.

Grandmother shook her head. "I had no idea it would be this difficult."

"I have a suggestion," offered Eliza. "Why don't we vote on the third girl?"

Grandmother's lips puckered as she considered this, but then she nodded. "Perhaps Eliza is right."

"I nominate Haley Callahan," said DJ quickly. "She's worked hard, and she's pretty and coordinated, and I think it would mean a lot to her to go with us." And just like that all the hands shot up.

"Goodness . . . it seems to be unanimous." Grandmother looked slightly worried. "But she is rather short, don't you think?"

"You mean petite," said Kriti.

"You said that Dylan wants real-looking models," said DJ.

Now Grandmother looked even more uncomfortable.

"And maybe it will be more balanced having two petite girls in our group," suggested Eliza.

Grandmother slowly nodded. "Yes, Eliza, I think you make a good point. All right, you girls will have your way. Haley it is."

Everyone clapped. Even DJ, although she suddenly realized that Haley, being the third choice, probably wouldn't be going anyway. Not with Taylor back in the game. Poor Haley. This was something DJ hadn't fully considered before.

"Now, if you'll excuse me," said Grandmother. "I have some things to prepare for class."

"Whew," said Rhiannon as Grandmother was gone. "That was close."

"We did it!" Casey made a hand-pump motion.

"Just say no to Madison," said Eliza triumphantly.

"New York, here we come," said Rhiannon.

"I can't believe we get to miss school for this," added Casey.

DJ didn't say anything. Mostly she just felt bad for Haley. Then again, it's not like Haley had been expecting to be picked. And if she didn't know she'd been a finalist, well, what difference would it make? More importantly, they had escaped any possibility of having Madison along.

The girls gathered as usual on the third floor. Naturally they asked Casey about her purplish blue hair, as well as Daisy, now sporting a jaunty little plaid hat to cover hers—Eliza's suggestion. Madison and Tina managed to appear as surprised as anyone, which DJ assumed was simply a well-rehearsed act. The session began, and Grandmother showed them a sneak preview DVD to Dylan's fall collection. But the whole time, DJ kept glancing nervously toward the door, hoping that Taylor would soon make her appearance.

"And today we will be taking measurements," Grandmother said after the DVD ended. "So that the appropriate clothing can be selected for the models who have been chosen to go to New York. I promised to get this information to Dylan today." There was a quiet murmuring in the crowd, and it was clear that everyone was eager to know who was going to Fashion Week.

Grandmother put her hands together and smiled. "And that means it's time to announce which lucky models will make their big New York debut next week. And I have a little surprise for you ... everyone who is chosen will have their way paid—that includes train fare, hotel, food, and other expenses."

The girls all let out an excited cheer, and then the room got quiet. DJ tried not to be obvious as she glanced back at the door again. Still no sign of Taylor. What if something had gone wrong? What if Taylor had already fallen off the wagon and gotten wasted last night? It could happen.

"As I'm sure you all know, the Carter House girls are my first choices. After all, they are the ones that Dylan originally invited. So to start with, I would like for the Carter House girls to come forward and line up, please."

DJ and the others went forward, lining up on the catwalk and waiting.

"As for the other three girls ..." Grandmother made a dramatic pause, and DJ stared at the door, actually praying now that Taylor would suddenly march in and make her big entrance. But no one was there.

"I need a drum roll." Grandmother chuckled as one of the girls imitated a drum roll. "Ariel Buford, please, come forward." Ariel looked shocked and pleased as she stood and joined them. "Daisy Kempton, please, you too have been selected." Daisy let out a happy yelp. "And Eliza has assured me that your hair and skin will be perfectly normal in a few days." Daisy giggled as she clumped onto the catwalk and stood beside Eliza. Just then DJ noticed dark frowns appearing on both Tina and Madison's faces. "And finally, we will be joined by Haley Callahan."

Haley jumped to her feet. "Me? Did you say me?" Her eyes were bright with hopeful happiness, and suddenly DJ felt really concerned. What would happen when Taylor showed up? Or would Taylor even show up? Either scenario seemed packed full of potential problems.

Grandmother smiled and nodded at Haley. "Yes, dear, I said your name." Haley came quickly forward, stood next to DJ, and even grabbed her hand and gave it a squeeze. DJ looked out on the girls remaining in their seats. There were only seven girls left, and every face looked genuinely disappointed. Not for the first time, DJ felt irked at this whole business. Why did Grandmother allow these girls to be set up like this, only to be let down later? Oh, she was sure that Grandmother would say, "That's the way it is in real life. Why should this be any different?" But did Grandmother really understand that issues like self-esteem and confidence were at stake here? Did she even care?

"And I do have a bit of good news for you girls who aren't going on this trip with us ..." Grandmother held her hands out wide. "You have all been invited to model in a spring fashion show at the country club in May. It will be a marvelous local event, and I hope you will all participate."

143

The girls sort of nodded and smiled, but DJ could tell this was small consolation compared to Fashion Week in New York City.

"Not only that," continued Grandmother. "But if Fashion Week becomes a tradition for Carter House, you will all have a chance of being chosen for the next Fashion Week as well. Isn't that wonderful?"

Their enthusiasm grew ever so slightly. But Grandmother seemed oblivious to the possibility of hurt feelings as she got them busy taking each other's measurements and filling out forms that would be sent to Dylan's design studio. But as they were doing this, all DJ could think about was *where was Taylor?* And the more she thought about it, the more convinced she became that something had gone wrong. Maybe Taylor had been lonely and called Seth last night. Maybe they'd gone out partying ... and maybe Taylor was right back where she'd been just a month ago. Finally, DJ couldn't stand another minute of not knowing. As soon as Rhiannon finished measuring her, DJ hurried to a quiet corner and pulled out her cell phone. She was just pressing the numbers when she heard Casey shrieking.

"*Taylor!*" she cried. "You're back!"

DJ turned in time to see Taylor coming in the door. The room actually grew hushed as everyone turned to see her walking in. To DJ's relief she didn't look wasted at all. In fact, she looked fantastic—like a rock star—as she strolled into the room. She was wearing what looked like a very expensive suit, kind of a caramel brown with safari pockets and a stunning braided leather belt and very cool shoes with killer heels. Soon they were all gathered around her, oohing and ahhing and complimenting her beautiful outfit. Everyone except Eliza.

She was standing over by the catwalk with a slight scowl playing across her high forehead.

"Welcome back," said Grandmother happily.

Casey and Rhiannon both hugged Taylor, and DJ just grinned as she joined them. "You made it," she said quietly to Taylor.

"Is that a Marc Jacobs?" Grandmother asked as she closely examined Taylor's suit.

Taylor smiled. "You nailed it, Mrs. Carter. But how did you know?"

Grandmother smiled with pride. "Just years of paying attention." Then she put an arm around Taylor's shoulders. "Oh, I'm so glad that you're back with us, dear. And just in time for the fashion show too."

"So who is going to be left behind now?" asked Eliza as she pressed her way into the circle of friends and observers that had surrounded Taylor. "Since it seems that Taylor is going to New York ... although she hasn't been to a single training session." Eliza looked directly at Grandmother now. "And you did say that only girls who had attended the sessions could go with us, *didn't you*, Mrs. Carter?"

Without even blinking, Grandmother waved her hand. "Surely, you know that doesn't apply to Taylor. Good grief, she already knows how to do the walk perfectly. And, as always, she looks stunning." Grandmother turned to Taylor. "Oh, Dylan will be so pleased to hear you're joining us."

"But you said only *eight* girls," persisted Eliza.

"Yes." Grandmother's brow creased. "That's true. Dylan wanted only eight girls for the show." She turned to Haley now. "I'm terribly sorry, Haley. But since you were the last pick ... well, in light of this unexpected occurrence, oh, I'm sure you'll understand why I must change my mind."

Haley nodded, but DJ thought she could see Haley's chin quiver just slightly. "I understand."

"Well, I don't understand," snapped Madison. "I think it's totally unfair that we go to all this work, we come to every class, we practice and do everything you ask, and then Taylor waltzes in and takes over like she owns the place." Then Madison grabbed Tina by the arm. "And we're like so outta here."

"Well." Grandmother just shook her head. "I'm sorry, girls."

"Don't let those two get to you," said Casey.

"I don't know," said Eliza. "I think Tina and Madison make a good point." Then she turned and walked out too.

"My goodness!" Grandmother blinked. "It seems emotions are running rampant today." She looked at her watch. "I think we'll do a few more runs down the catwalk and call it a day, girls. I find all this emotion to be exhausting."

Taylor slipped into the lineup and did her walk just as easily and naturally as ever. Like she'd been doing it her whole life. Grandmother actually clapped when she finished. "Yes, just like that, girls. Pay attention to Taylor. No one does it half as well as she does."

And it was true; no one else in their group could do the walk quite like Taylor. But, unlike times in the past when Taylor had come across as somewhat haughty and arrogant, today she seemed changed. Now as Taylor strutted down the catwalk, something was different. DJ wondered if the others could see it too. Oh, sure, Taylor still held her head high and her shoulders back. But there was a new softness about her, the same thing that DJ had noticed yesterday—the same thing that had worried DJ slightly. But now, rather than seeming like a flaw or a deficiency, DJ thought it made Taylor look better than ever.

14

New York Debut

AS THE "CHOSEN" GIRLS CONTINUED to practice the cat-walk, DJ observed that, one by one, Haley and the rest of the girls who hadn't been picked were quietly slipping out of the room. They reminded DJ of whipped animals with their tails tucked between their legs, trying to get out without being seen. Very sad.

And, although DJ was hugely relieved that Taylor had made it and seemed perfectly fine, she felt sorry for the others. Okay, maybe not Madison and Tina so much. Mostly she felt badly for Haley—to raise and then dash her hopes all within a short time seemed unusually cruel. And, not for the first time, DJ wondered why American culture put so much value in super-ficial things like physical appearance. Even more than that, she wondered why she was forced to be part of it.

Finally, the practice session was winding down, and DJ knew what she had to do. She had made a decision, and as she marched over to her grandmother, she knew that nothing was going to dissuade her from it.

"Grandmother," she said firmly. "May I have a word with you?"

"Certainly, Desiree. Is something wrong?"

"Yes. I would like to step down from the fashion show."

"*What?*" Grandmother's pale blue eyes glinted with fire now.

"I'd like to offer my spot to Haley Callahan. She desperately wants to go. And you know that I'm not that interested in this sort—"

"*Not interested?*" Grandmother's hand came up to her chest as if she expected to have a heart attack. "You're not interested in participating in one of the biggest fashion shows of the year, Desiree?"

"That's right. I'd like Haley to go in my place."

Grandmother just shook her head. "Oh, Desiree ..."

"Please, Grandmother. Haley wants to go so badly. I know she's brokenhearted right now. Please, I'm begging you to let her go instead of me."

Grandmother sighed then shrugged. "Fine, Desiree. Although I do not agree, and I fear you will regret it, I will let you make this decision."

"Thank you!" DJ actually hugged her stunned grandmother, then hurried to dial Haley's number, waiting impatiently for her to answer.

"Guess what?" DJ cried.

"What?" Haley's voice sounded flat and discouraged.

"You're going to New York!"

"I don't think so ..."

"No, you are, Haley. I just talked to Grandmother and—"

"No way. Taylor made that—"

"Trust me, Haley. You *are* going! Grandmother wants you back in the show." Okay, maybe that wasn't one hundred percent true. But it was sort of true since she'd said DJ could choose.

"Really?" Haley's voice was laced with hope now.

"Absolutely."

"Oh, that's so great, DJ. Thank you! Thank you!"

Just as DJ finished the conversation and hung up, she felt someone tapping her on the shoulder. She turned to see Taylor looking at her with a perplexed expression.

"What did you just do?" asked Taylor.

DJ confessed that she'd given her spot to Haley. "With Grandmother's approval."

"Why?"

"Because Haley was brokenhearted."

"That's my fault, isn't it?"

"No ..." DJ firmly shook her head. "It's just the way it happened."

"But I want *you* to go to New York."

DJ shrugged. "Sorry." Then she considered something. "Hey, don't tell the others I'm not going, okay?" She could imagine Casey getting mad at her or Rhiannon trying to talk her into it. DJ didn't need that.

Taylor frowned, but at least she agreed. "Okay, mum's the word. At least for the moment. Anyway, I have something else to ask you about."

"What?"

"Is it true ..." Taylor lowered her voice, "that I'm now rooming with Princess Eliza?"

DJ grimaced. "Oh, yeah, I almost forgot. Sorry."

Taylor firmly shook her head. "I cannot do that. Seriously, DJ, I'd rather sleep on the floor somewhere else than be with Eliza. Rooming with Eliza would probably put me right back to where I was. I just can't do it. I'm sorry."

DJ explained the problem with Kriti and Grandmother's decision to switch rooms. "It's not like I really had a choice."

"I know. And I feel sorry for Kriti. It's no surprise that Eliza has messed with the poor girl's mind. And it's not that I couldn't stand up to Eliza, it's just that I don't need that kind of stress in my life right now. Do you understand?"

"Totally. I'm just not sure what we can do. I hate to send Kriti back to Eliza. I mean, she's trying to knock off the anorexia game, but she's not out of the woods yet, if you know what I mean."

Taylor nodded. "Not only do I know what you mean, I'm there too."

"So what should we do?"

"I don't know." Taylor looked really sad now. "I just wish I was rooming with you again, DJ. You're the only one in this house who really understands me."

DJ felt surprisingly touched by this admission, but she tried not to show it. "Let me see what I can do about it."

"Thanks." Taylor smiled. "In the meantime, I need to pick up my bags from the B&B. It's only a couple of blocks, but I've got a lot —"

"You can use my car if you want." DJ went over to where their things were stashed on the chairs and quickly fished her car keys out of her purse, then handed them to Taylor.

Taylor smiled down at the Gucci bag. "Hey, you're still using it."

DJ held up the pretty bag. "Do you want it back?"

"No, of course not. I think it's more you than me."

After Taylor left, DJ explained the dilemma to Rhiannon. "I think if it was anyone but Eliza, Taylor might be okay. But Eliza would probably give Taylor an excuse to start drinking again."

Rhiannon frowned. "It's like my mom says, any excuse is a good excuse to use when you're an addict."

"I know that's probably true," admitted DJ. "But in the case of Taylor and Eliza . . . well, it's kind of predictable. I saw the two of them in Vegas, and it wasn't healthy for either of them."

"So what do you suggest we do?" asked Rhiannon. "You're not suggesting that Kriti go back with Eliza, are you?"

"Not at all. Especially not right before Fashion Week," agreed DJ. "Kriti already seems to be teetering on the edge as it is."

"I wish Eliza would get a clue and start treating people better." Rhiannon pushed a stray auburn curl away from her forehead.

"I suppose I could room with her," said DJ slowly. "And then Taylor could be with Kriti."

"But didn't you say Taylor wants to room with you?"

"Yeah, but we don't always get what we want, do we?"

"But how do you think Kriti would feel about rooming with Taylor? Talk about your opposites."

DJ shrugged. "Taylor has changed."

"There's only one thing to do." Rhiannon put her hands on her hips and nodded. "I will room with Eliza."

DJ frowned. "Are you serious?"

"Totally."

Now Rhiannon started to chuckle. "I'll consider it my *mission*. Remember last week's sermon about how each one of us has our own special mission field, but we don't usually know where it's located."

"Even so, that's a big sacrifice, Rhiannon. I hope you don't regret it."

"And it appears that Taylor is your mission. And it seems like you're doing a good job."

DJ thought that was a stretch. "Thanks, but I haven't done anything."

Rhiannon's mouth twisted into a half smile. "So Kriti can move in with Casey, and Taylor can have her bed back."

"Great."

Rhiannon poked DJ. "But *you* get to tell Casey about the switch."

"That seems fair enough." Although DJ wasn't looking forward to informing Casey that they'd agreed on this without her consent. But as it turned out, Casey was fairly understanding.

"So you really don't mind?" DJ asked.

"To be honest, when you first started talking about this, I was afraid I was going to be stuck with Eliza. And that could get ugly."

DJ laughed. "I'm sure you're relieved that it's Rhiannon going into the lion's den."

"If anyone can handle that lion, it's Rhiannon." Casey looked a little sad now. "But I'll admit that I'll miss her."

"But I think Kriti will appreciate getting to know you better, Casey. You might even be good for her."

"Hey, maybe she'll help me with my homework."

By the time Taylor made it back to Carter House with her bags, DJ had informed Kriti about the change in rooms. "I hope you don't mind," she told her. "But Taylor really wants her room back."

"I understand." Kriti focused on gathering up some of her things. "You and Taylor seem to have a good friendship."

DJ kind of laughed. "Well, it's an unusual one anyway."

"I figured this was just temporary anyway." Kriti's back was to DJ as she slipped her laptop into a case along with some other books. Suddenly DJ was worried that Kriti was feeling hurt.

"Casey is really nice," said DJ quickly. "She's looking forward to getting to know you better. You're okay with it, aren't you?"

Kriti turned and looked at DJ with wide dark eyes. "The truth is I'm just relieved not to be going back with Eliza. Ironic, since I remember how furious I was when Mrs. Carter told me she wanted me to switch roommates. I suppose it really was for the best."

DJ almost mentioned that Casey would probably be a good influence when it came to eating too since, after DJ, Casey had the biggest appetite in Carter House. Still, DJ didn't want to push it. Instead, she helped Kriti to gather her things.

"What is going on?" demanded Eliza when she saw DJ and Kriti carrying a load of Kriti's belongings across the hallway.

DJ quickly explained the switches.

"I suppose I'm the last to know about this." Eliza frowned at DJ.

"Apparently."

"Well, at least Rhiannon won't have as much junk as Taylor," snapped Eliza. "I'll appreciate it if Taylor gets her things out of my room ASAP."

DJ just nodded. But she chuckled to herself as she considered what Eliza's reaction might be when she saw all of Rhiannon's rag-tag retro collection of clothes and fabric and things arriving in her room. Plus DJ would encourage Rhiannon to use her fair share of closet space too!

The next few days felt like a whirlwind of emotions and controversies and chaos to DJ. It seemed the competition between the girls was only intensifying. More than ever, she felt thankful that she wouldn't be an actual participant in the big fashion show. Not that she'd tipped her hand to anyone. Well, besides

Taylor, and although she wasn't happy about DJ's decision, she could be trusted to keep her mouth shut.

By Monday Casey and Daisy, following their weekend of hair appointments, exfoliating facials, and various dye-removing formulas, had nearly erased the effects of the blue dye job—a huge relief since they hadn't looked forward to being teased at school. During the weekend, Eliza had been calling Casey an "overgrown Smurf girl" until everyone had gotten sick of it. At lunch time, DJ couldn't help but smile as she noticed Madison and Tina's disappointment to see that Daisy and Casey looked just fine. As if to rub it in, Daisy and Casey intentionally strutted right past the other girls' table. DJ just hoped that Madison and Tina weren't planning some other form of sabotage.

But it was Taylor's return from rehab that caused the biggest buzz at school. As usual, rumors were flying right and left, but Taylor acted totally nonchalant, like *no big deal*, like no one was talking and like she hadn't been gone at all. DJ wasn't even sure how she managed to pull this off, but she had to admire it. Then, on Tuesday, the buzz around Taylor got even louder when she publicly broke up with Seth in the cafeteria. Everyone knew that Seth had been acting like a great big jerk while Taylor was gone. And whether it was right or wrong, DJ thoroughly enjoyed watching him being cut down to size in front of everyone. It took great self-control not to stand and cheer as she watched the drama unfold.

"I wouldn't want you to be stuck with a loser like me," Taylor told Seth with a slight twinkle in her eye. "I'm sure it must be so embarrassing for you to have a girlfriend like me ... having been in rehab and all. You should go find yourself someone who deserves a *great* guy like you." Seth was pretty much speechless. And Taylor, looking more beautiful than ever, just shook her head and said, "See ya later, dude" and walked away. DJ wanted to cheer.

As the week progressed, it seemed the Carter House girls and Fashion Week had become the talk of the town. They made both the local paper and school paper and were even interviewed by Channel Five News, airing on Wednesday evening. Naturally, Madison and Tina went around telling everyone that Mrs. Carter's modeling sessions were rigged and that she should be sued. Tina's father (an attorney) was probably looking into it right now. Not that DJ or the others were taking these threats seriously. But it did seem that everyone was slightly on edge. Particularly the recently dethroned Eliza.

Naturally, she had not been the least bit pleased that Taylor had made it back in time for Fashion Week. On Wednesday morning, her usual saccharine southern charm completely evaporated when Grandmother complimented not only Taylor's new outfit, but her makeup and hair as well.

"Taylor is setting a new standard for Carter House," Grandmother had gushed in front of everyone at the breakfast table. "The *gold* standard."

"Perhaps we all need a lockdown in an alcohol rehabilitation facility to learn more about fashion and style," Eliza said snidely.

Grandmother pretended to ignore this mean comment, but DJ could tell that it had registered anyway. She suspected that it hadn't elevated Eliza in Grandmother's mind. That was enough to give DJ hope that her grandmother wasn't quite as shallow as she sometimes appeared.

But Taylor wasn't the only bee in Miss Eliza's bonnet. Eliza was also grumbling about her new roommate. She did not appreciate "Preacher Girl," as she liked to call Rhiannon. What she didn't know was that the harder she made life for Rhiannon, the more sermons, Christian music, and Bible quoting she'd get in return. Rhiannon had a plan.

But Rhiannon and Taylor weren't solely to blame for Eliza's bad temper. It seemed that something else was brewing as well. At first, DJ thought she'd imagined it, but now she was pretty certain that Harry was developing a serious interest in Taylor. Oddly enough considering her history, it hadn't been instigated by Taylor this time. Not that she had ceased to flirt with guys, which was strangely relieving, but this thing with Harry had seemed to start rather innocently. DJ had witnessed the whole thing. It happened the day after Taylor's public breakup with Seth. Harry had politely asked Taylor about rehab, and she admitted that it had been her idea to go in.

"Seriously?" he questioned her. "I heard that you'd gotten into trouble with the law and that rehab was part of your sentencing." He glanced at Eliza now, as if perhaps she was the source of this misinformation.

Taylor looked curiously at Eliza, but received only a chilly blank stare in return. "No one forced me into rehab," Taylor told Harry. Everyone at the lunch table was suddenly all ears.

"So what was it then?" he persisted. "What made you decide to turn yourself in?"

DJ was tempted to jump in, to say something to change the subject, to crack a joke, to protect Taylor somehow. But Taylor, as usual, needed no protection.

"I was out of control," Taylor said simply. "And a good friend helped me to see that." She smiled at DJ now.

"Do you mean you're never going to drink again?" Harry looked skeptical. "I mean, you were pretty into partying, Taylor. Are you saying you were able to just stop cold turkey, and that's it?"

"I'm saying it's a one-day-at-a-time kind of thing," she explained. "Like I know I'm not going to drink today. But tomorrow I'll have to make up my mind all over again."

"Just like those old twelve-step rules?"

"That's exactly right." She grinned. "Not that glamorous, is it?"

"But your rehab place was in Malibu, right? Was it some kind of a celebrity joint?"

Taylor laughed. "I'm not giving out names, but let's just say it was interesting. A diverse crowd of needy people ... all there for basically the same reason."

"But you'd recommend this place?"

Taylor looked directly into Harry's eyes now—probably the very gesture that made Eliza slam down her salad fork and glare at the two of them. Judging by Eliza's expression, you'd think that Harry and Taylor were locking lips rather than just talking.

"Absolutely," Taylor assured Harry. "I'd recommend rehab treatment to anyone who needs it and is up for the challenge. But don't assume that it's an easy thing to do, Harry."

He shook his head. "I didn't think it was."

"It takes guts. Getting and staying sober is hard work. And once you realize you need it ... you're the only one who can make it happen."

Apparently Eliza was fed up by then. Because that's when she stormed off. Okay, she didn't exactly storm. She simply stood and gracefully walked away—without saying a word to anyone. But DJ had observed the look in her eyes, and it seemed pretty certain that a storm was brewing. It was anyone's guess when Hurricane Eliza was going to hit.

15

New York Debut

FINALLY IT WAS THURSDAY—the big day. After school, they would gather their bags and head off to the Big Apple. Well, everyone except for DJ.

Grandmother had gone over all the tedious details the evening before, giving them printouts of their schedule for the next few days, as well as maps of the city and guidelines for their behavior, etc., etc. DJ had been relieved not to listen.

But now it was morning, and Grandmother had yet another "important announcement" to make before they left the breakfast table.

"As you girls know we'll be taking the five o'clock train into the city today. But I have a surprise." She glanced directly at DJ now. "You may have heard that Desiree has opted to stay behind so that Haley Callahan could go in her place to New York and—"

"Actually, I hadn't told them." DJ knew she'd interrupted her Grandmother, a cardinal no-no, but she wanted to set the record straight. And now all eyes were on her.

"What's up with that?" sputtered Casey with a mouthful of granola.

159

"Manners!" Grandmother shook her finger at her.

"DJ, you *have* to go with us," complained Rhiannon. "I was hoping that you'd go to the design studio with me."

"I'm sorry." DJ just looked down at her plate.

"You gave up your spot for Haley Callahan?" demanded Eliza. "How stupid was that?"

"It was *not* stupid," said Taylor. "DJ was simply being kind to Haley. Remember what *kind* is like, Eliza? Or has that four letter word been eradicated from your vocabulary?"

"That was a real sacrifice, DJ," said Kriti with admiration.

"It's not like it was a huge sacrifice," DJ said quietly. "I mean, everyone knows that I'm not into the fashion scene. I'll be perfectly happy to stay home and—"

"Enough!" Grandmother held up her hands to stop them. "As I was trying to say, I have an important announcement to make. And it is not that Desiree is *not* going to New York. If I could get a word in edgewise, I would inform everyone that Desiree is going with us after all."

"I am?" DJ wasn't sure whether to be glad or mad. "Why?"

"First of all, I explained our little dilemma to Dylan last night," Grandmother continued. "And he insisted that Desiree must participate in Fashion Week. He still remembers how you fell at the last fashion show and what a wonderful recovery you and Taylor made as you did the walk. But I explained to him about your concern for your friend Haley. And so he has agreed to have *nine* girls in his show." Grandmother beamed at DJ now. "Isn't that wonderful?"

Wonderful or not, DJ was feeling slightly stunned as they all piled onto the train a little before five o'clock. And to her surprise she was actually rather happy that she'd been included. Even more surprising was the fact that a number of their friends from school had come to the train station to see them off. And not just their boyfriends, although they were there too. But the news people were there again and even the girls from Grandmother's Saturday sessions had shown up. Not Tina and Madison, of course. They were probably in Tina's father's office writing up some big lawsuit.

"Knock 'em dead in New York," said Conner as he planted a kiss firmly on DJ's cheek.

"So you forgive me for breaking our date tonight?" she asked as he handed her overnight bag to her.

"As long as you don't go and sign with some mega-modeling agency in New York."

She rolled her eyes. "Yeah, right."

"As long as we're still on for next Friday."

"For sure."

"And while I've got you agreeing to everything … how about going to the Valentine's dance with me too?"

She just grinned. "Okay, you talked me into it."

"Hurry now, girls," called Grandmother. "We still need to go through security."

"You go, girls!" yelled Haley's mom as she waved with tears in her eyes.

"Come on, ladies," Grandmother was herding them toward the security gate now. "Let's not miss our train. It's time to go now."

"Move it along," urged Inez. Grandmother had brought Inez to help keep the nine girls in line. A nice gesture, but DJ imagined Inez would be pulling her hair out before the weekend was over.

Before long, they were all seated, and as the train pulled out of town, DJ sat and studied this interesting assortment of girls—girls who wouldn't have known each other or chosen to sit together just a year ago. Eliza and Daisy were looking at

161

the latest *Vogue*. As usual, Eliza was playing princess, and her new handmaid, Daisy was liberally doling out the devotion and loyalty expected of her. Across from them sat Haley and Ariel and Kriti, chatting away like they'd been best friends for ages. DJ wasn't even sure what had connected those three. Maybe it was their height, or lack of, but it would probably be good for Kriti. Plus, it was a relief to see them sharing a bag of "carb-filled" chips and drinking "sugar-laden" sodas. Hopefully Grandmother wasn't watching.

Kriti seemed to enjoy Haley and Ariel's attention as she told them about her dad's designer reproduction business in the city. She even showed off her fake Hermes bag that could easily pass for the real deal in most circles. Haley and Ariel were both eager to see Kriti's dad's store, and Kriti promised to take them there tomorrow.

"I wouldn't mind looking at the knockoffs too," said Taylor from behind them.

"Me too," said Rhiannon.

"Everyone can come." Kriti's dark eyes sparkled happily.

"Everyone who wants to settle for fake bags," said Eliza snootily. Daisy said nothing, but DJ suspected by her expression that she would easily settle if Eliza wasn't looking.

"Not everyone is dumb enough to waste hundreds of dollars for silly designer names," countered Casey.

Eliza just glared at her, then turned back around and whispered something to Daisy. Naturally, Daisy laughed. Poor Daisy.

"When I become a famous designer ..." Rhiannon giggled, "I'll make sure that my clothing stays affordable for everyone."

The chatter went on back and forth, and DJ realized that she was really glad that she'd been able to come. Despite her whining and complaining about obsessed fashion freaks, it was fun to be here with her friends and on their way to New York. She would have to remember to thank Grandmother—and Dylan—for including her.

It was getting close to seven when they finally arrived at Grand Central, and the terminal was alive with color and motion as if the whole place was abuzz with Fashion Week. There were banners advertising the various designers and events, and a flurry of people coming and going, all seeming to have some connection to Fashion Week. DJ thought she could feel the electricity in the air—and once again, she was glad she'd come.

Grandmother had ordered two stretch limos. Inez gathered up Haley, Ariel, Kriti, Rhiannon, and Casey into one of the cars. DJ and the others went with Grandmother.

"I feel like a celebrity," said Daisy as she leaned back into the seat and sighed loudly. "Or like I'm still dreaming." She laughed. "Don't wake me up!"

"I love New York," said Taylor. "Even though I'm a West Coast girl by birth. I still love New York."

Eliza didn't say anything. Instead, she stared down at her cell phone as if she expected it to ring. Rumor had it that Harry had just broken up with her, but no one wanted to ask. The other rumor was that Harry already had his eye on Taylor. And that didn't surprise DJ a bit, especially after she'd seen him watching Taylor at lunch today. Fortunately, Taylor had seemed oblivious and, naturally, DJ didn't mention it. Still, she knew it would only spell trouble. But hopefully, it was trouble that they wouldn't have to deal with until they went home.

"The garment district is in Manhattan, otherwise known as Midtown," Grandmother informed them, acting as if she was their tour guide. "The other two districts are Uptown and Downtown."

"How do you know which is which?" asked Daisy.

"Uptown is north of Midtown, and Downtown is south."

"Oh." Daisy nodded, but still looked confused.

"Don't worry about it, Daisy," snapped Eliza. "I know my way around well enough. We won't get lost."

"No one should get lost," Grandmother informed them. "You have your maps, and your feet or the subway can get you almost everywhere you want to go."

"What about taxis?" asked Daisy.

"Good luck," said Grandmother. "Don't forget this is Fashion Week. A very busy time. Often you can get where you're going much faster on foot."

"Unless you're wearing four-inch heels." Eliza held up a red strappy shoe. "And, trust me, these Christian Louboutins are not made for hiking."

"That's why I told you girls to carry a spare pair of running shoes in your bags," Grandmother reminded her.

Eliza made an innocent face. *Running* shoes?"

"Yes," said DJ dryly, "those are shoes that are specially designed to *run*."

"Here we are," announced Grandmother.

"Already?" Daisy looked reluctant to leave the stretch limo.

"We weren't that far from the train station," DJ explained. "We could've walked if we didn't have luggage."

"*Some* people could've walked," said Eliza as she got out of the limo. "Not anyone with any class."

"You mean the remedial class?" teased Taylor.

DJ laughed. Okay, maybe she shouldn't encourage Taylor, but it was nice to see that Taylor still knew how to bring Eliza back to reality. She'd missed that.

Grandmother smiled up at the old-looking building. "The Carlton isn't the fanciest Manhattan hotel, but it's my favorite."

Eliza frowned. "I thought we were staying at the Bryant Park Hotel."

Grandmother blinked. "What made you think that?"

"Isn't that where the models stay?"

Grandmother laughed in a rather dismissive way. "Oh, my. You girls have so much to learn about the fashion world."

The other girls' limo arrived, and soon all nine girls, Grandmother, Inez, and their luggage were spilling out onto the sidewalk. Several bellhops rushed toward them with big smiles and oversized carts to load the luggage on.

"Isn't this wonderful," said Rhiannon as they went inside the lobby.

"I've never been in New York," Casey admitted to DJ. "But I thought it was bigger than this."

Kriti laughed. "You know, I said that exact same thing when we moved here. I mean, it's certainly big, but the buildings are so close . . . the streets are so narrow, and Manhattan is really not all that large. It's kind of a small sort of big, you know?"

"That's true," said Taylor.

The girls explored the luxurious but crowded lobby as Grandmother registered them for their rooms. The place had an old-world sort of elegance, and DJ decided that she liked it. Much better than the huge modern hotel they'd stayed at in Vegas. Inez was calling to the girls now. "Come, come," she commanded. "Mrs. Carter wants a word with you."

Grandmother gathered the girls around her in a semiquiet corner near the elevators. "I know that I've already lectured you about manners, decorum, and representing yourselves as ladies, but I just want to remind you that I will not tolerate any nonsense." She looked directly at Eliza now. "And absolutely no alcohol." She glanced at Taylor too. "Is that understood?"

"Totally," said Taylor with a smile.

"Of course," said Eliza a bit meekly.

"Good." Grandmother held up several key cards now. "I have put Eliza, Daisy, and Kriti in one room. You girls can figure out how you will share the two queen beds." She handed the key cards to Eliza, and DJ had no doubts that Princess Eliza would be the one to have a bed to herself.

"In the adjoining room will be Desiree and Taylor." She handed them both a key. Then she looked directly at DJ. "I will be in the room next to yours. Not adjoining, but close enough. I'll expect you to take the role of a junior chaperone, Desiree."

"Me?" DJ frowned.

Grandmother nodded, then turned her attention to the other girls. "And Casey, Rhiannon, Haley, and Ariel will share a room across the hallway. Inez will be your chaperone, and since she prefers to sleep alone, I have ordered her a roll-away bed, which I was told is quite comfortable. Any questions?" Grandmother smiled. "Good. Now, your bags should be in your rooms. And, if you've looked at the schedule I gave you girls, you will know when and where we are meeting for dinner. Until then ..."

Suddenly they were all scrambling for elevators, waiting in lines, and crowding in here and there when they got the chance. As it turned out, Eliza, DJ, and Taylor found themselves crammed into a corner as they rode up to the twenty-third floor.

"How do you rate?" Eliza's voice was quiet, but with an edge.

"Huh?" DJ peered curiously at her.

Eliza nodded to Taylor, "You two getting a room to yourselves?"

DJ shrugged. "So?"

"So . . . why are you two so special? The only ones to get a whole room with two beds to yourself."

"Just lucky, I guess."

"Or maybe DJ set it up special with Grandma-ma." Now Eliza's voice sounded as if she was suggesting something.

"What are you inferring?" asked Taylor.

Eliza got a slightly wicked smile. "Oh, I don't know . . ."

It was time to get off the elevator, but DJ was still curious. "What are you trying to say, Eliza?"

"Oh . . . well, you two shared a room in Vegas together. You had to be roommates when Taylor got back. And now you have to have a private room and no one else does . . . I guess some people might draw some conclusions . . ."

"Such as?" Taylor turned to face Eliza.

"You know . . . and, trust me, I'm an open-minded person. I have no problems with sexual preferences."

"What?" demanded DJ. "What are you insinuating?"

"Nothing . . . nothing at all." Eliza gave them her sugary sweet smile. Then just as she slid her key card into the lock, the other girls came down the hallway, laughing and joking about some guy who had hit on Daisy in the elevator.

"Eliza is such a witch," said Taylor as they went into their room.

"She's just jealous," said DJ as she picked one of her bags from the small heap on the floor, tossing it onto the queen bed nearest the door.

"Jealous of who?"

"You, of course."

"And that would be because of . . . ?"

"Harry, for one thing. You know that he broke up with Eliza, don't you?"

"Everyone knows that."

"And now he seems to be looking at you."

"Hey, I've done nothing to encourage—"

"You didn't have to."

Taylor swore as she tossed a bag onto the other bed.

"Just be warned, Taylor. Eliza may be on the warpath."

"And that's news?"

DJ laughed, but at the same time wasn't so sure that it was all that funny. Hopefully Eliza wouldn't do anything stupid … anything that might spoil Fashion Week for the others. Because, as strange as it seemed, DJ had suddenly started to care about how everything turned out in New York. And the reason she cared was as much for her grandmother's sake as it was for the girls who really wanted to be here.

16

New York Debut

"I am going shopping today," Eliza proclaimed as they finished up breakfast in the hotel restaurant.

"Just don't forget to be at Dylan's studio at one o'clock sharp." Grandmother finished signing the bill, then stood. "I promised him that we'll be at his complete disposal until five for all the last-minute fittings and adjustments."

"I won't forget," promised Rhiannon. "I'm already counting the minutes until I'm actually in a real design studio."

"I'm counting the minutes until I'll be in a real fashion show," added Daisy.

"Not just a fashion show," Grandmother corrected. "Fashion Week!" She smiled at the girls. "Now does everyone remember what I said about staying together? I don't want any of you traipsing about the city by yourselves, is that perfectly clear?"

They all said yes, and then Grandmother reminded them to keep their cell phones on. "And have a pleasant morning. The weather seems to be cooperating with us today." Then she hurried over to a nearby table where she was heartily greeted and welcomed by what DJ guessed were some of her former fashion associates. DJ had been surprised at how many people had stopped her grandmother to say hello. And she hadn't missed how pleased Grandmother was when she was recognized. Or how proud she was to show off her girls. And, a couple of times she actually took the time to introduce her granddaughter. Although DJ didn't appreciate the bit about "aspiring model." That was the last thing DJ would ever aspire toward. But she had been polite and simply smiled. Let Grandmother enjoy her day in the sun. At her age, these little perks were probably becoming fewer and farther between.

"Back to shopping," said Eliza as the girls gathered their purses and jackets and things, getting ready to head off to see the city. "Who wants to go with me?"

"I do! I do!" Daisy giggled self-consciously now. "I mean, I don't have much money to spend, but I'd love to watch you spend yours."

Eliza smiled, then looked hopefully at the rest of the group. "Anyone else want to hit the big designer stores with me? I know where the best shopping places are, and I'll pay for the taxi."

But it seemed she had no other takers. "So what is everyone else doing this morning?" she ventured.

"I'm going to the Garment District," announced Rhiannon. "I want to see it all—from the Fashion Walk of Fame clear down to the last button shop." She laughed. "Or as much as I can see in a few hours."

"What about everyone else?" persisted Eliza. She looked directly at DJ now.

"Some of us are going with Rhiannon." DJ tried to sound low-key, but the truth was DJ and Taylor had already decided to go with Casey and Rhiannon to the Garment District in the hopes that they could put some space between themselves and

Eliza. After the way Eliza had been treating Taylor last night, it seemed the safest route.

"So you're *all* going with Rhiannon to the Garment District?" Eliza asked with a suspicious tone to her voice.

"Kriti's dad's company is there," said Haley. "We planned to do some back-room shopping there as well as getting the Garment District tour from Rhiannon."

"Rhiannon's giving tours now?" Eliza narrowed her eyes. "Why wasn't I invited?"

"It's not like invitations were sent out," said Casey.

"I just planned to go there." Rhiannon held up her map. "And a few others wanted to come along. You can come too if you like."

"But you better have on your running shoes," DJ pointed out. "We'll be covering a lot of turf."

Taylor looked down at Eliza's shoes and shook her head. "Sorry, but those Marc Jacobs are not going to cut it."

"Speaking of Marc Jacobs," said Eliza. "That's the first shop I'll be visiting." She made what seemed a forced smile. "Too bad you girls are going to miss out on it." Then she turned to Daisy. "Come on," she commanded. "The designers are calling."

"I hope I didn't hurt her feelings," said Rhiannon as they watched Eliza and Daisy hurrying through the lobby.

"Don't worry," said Casey. "She doesn't *have* feelings."

"I forgot to bring my purse down," said Ariel. "Do you mind waiting?"

"Just hurry," said Rhiannon. "We're burning daylight."

Of course, that's when Ariel realized she'd forgotten her camera in the room, and then Haley remembered she'd left her cell phone in the charger, and to top it off Kriti needed to use the restroom. Finally, after what felt like an hour to DJ, they were heading out of the hotel.

"Look at that," said Casey as she pointed to where Eliza and Daisy were standing near the curb. "They haven't even gotten a taxi yet."

"Hey, Eliza," called out Taylor as their group moved past the pair of girls. "You should've walked. You'd be there by now."

Eliza turned and sneered. "Thanks for the news flash."

Casey laughed, and DJ elbowed her.

"What?" demanded Casey.

"Why antagonize her?" said DJ quietly.

"Antagonize *her*?" Casey made a snooty face. "What about the rest of us?"

"It's just that she's already in a snit," said DJ. "Let's not push her, okay?"

But Casey just shook her head.

"Hurry," called Rhiannon. "Let's cross this street while we can!"

Rhiannon proved to be a good tour guide. Not only did she find her way through the Garment District, her knowledge of what went on there was rather impressive.

"This is the Fashion Walk of Fame," announced Rhiannon. "Look, there's Ralph Lauren's plaque."

"And Betsey Johnson," said Haley. "I like her designs."

"And here's Marc Jacobs," pointed out Casey. "You think Eliza will be jealous?"

DJ tossed Casey a look.

"This is Bonnie Cashin!" exclaimed Rhiannon as she stooped down to touch the plaque. "Wow!"

"Who is that?" asked DJ.

"Just one of the greatest American designers." Rhiannon sighed.

"How come we haven't heard of her?" asked Haley.

"I've heard of her," said Taylor. "She started out designing costumes for theater, I think."

Rhiannon stood up and stared at Taylor in surprise. "That's right. How did you know that?"

Taylor grinned. "I get around."

"She was an artist too," said Rhiannon. "But she was one of the best midcentury women designers. Anyone ever hear of Coach?"

"Of course," said Ariel. "My mom loves her Coach bag."

"Cashin pretty much launched Coach. But she did a lot more than that." Rhiannon went on to tell about how Cashin designed clothes that women actually wanted to wear, how she won lots of awards, and other trivia.

"How do you know all this?" asked DJ.

"Your grandmother gave me a book on her."

"Why?"

"Because I was wearing something that my great-aunt gave me — remember that plaid coat that I love. Well, your grandmother recognized it as a Cashin original. We got to talking, and it turned out that your grandmother actually knew her. They were very good friends."

"Were?"

"Bonnie Cashin passed away in 2000."

"Wow, you're a real Cashin expert," said Ariel.

Rhiannon nodded. "I really admire her work."

Next, Rhiannon took them to the Fashion Institute of Technology. "This is where I want to go to college," she told them. "It's pretty expensive, but Mrs. Carter is helping me to apply for scholarships and work-study programs." She crossed her fingers hopefully. "I know the odds are against me, but I'm praying for a miracle."

Before they knew it, it was noon. Kriti informed them there was no way they'd have time to visit her dad's company, have lunch, and make it to Dylan's by one. "But we can go tomorrow," she reassured them. "He's not as busy on Saturdays, and he can give us the full tour as well as shopping privileges."

Rhiannon paused by the fashion institute's museum entrance and sighed sadly. "There's not enough time to see this today either. But anyone who wants to join me tomorrow is welcome."

So it was agreed, they would spend the early part of the day exploring Kriti's father's company, the fashion museum, and the other "must-see" places, according to Rhiannon.

"And then it's practice for the fashion show," Ariel reminded them as she held up her schedule. "From two until five."

"And we'll all have Sunday off to do as we please," said DJ. "I plan to play the tourist. I want to go to the Statue of Liberty and the top of the Empire State Building and all sorts of goofy things. Anyone else?" She didn't mention that the last time she'd done these things had been with her mother—shortly after her parents' divorce and a couple of years before her mother died.

"I'm in," said Casey. "It's my first time in the Big Apple, and I'm willing to act like a tourist. I'll even ride in one of those silly double-decker buses if we can sit on top and wave at people."

Taylor laughed. "Okay, I'll come along too—as long as you promise we can go to the Museum of Modern Art."

"And Times Square," added Casey.

"You two sound like real tourists to me," teased DJ. "Anyone else want to come along and act like freaks?"

"Count me out," said Rhiannon. "I'm going to soak up every bit of the Garment District that I can. I want to eat, drink, and roll around in design, design, design."

"I'm with you," said Haley.

Ariel nodded. "Do you mind if I tag along?"

"Me too?" asked Kriti hopefully.

"Sounds like our weekend is all mapped out," said Rhiannon.

DJ hoped that Eliza and Daisy wouldn't feel left out. Maybe they'd want to join Rhiannon and the others in the Garment District tour. She felt fairly certain that Eliza wouldn't want to lower herself to playing tourist and riding around on a double-decker bus. And that was just fine with DJ.

They had a quick lunch at a Chinese restaurant that Kriti recommended. After that they hurried over to Dylan's design studio, arriving there a few minutes early, which made Rhiannon happy because she got to get a sneak peek at some of the inner workings. And then Dylan rounded them all up into the conference room to explain what exactly he expected from his models.

"As you know, I'm the new kid on the block," he told them. "Kind of like you girls. So naturally, I'm jazzed and nervous." He laughed. "I'm actually rather giddy."

"You will do just fine," Grandmother reassured him.

"I cannot tell you how much it means to have Katherine Carter in my court," he said to all of them. "It is huge." He turned to her. "Thank you so much for taking me under your wing."

She smiled happily. "It's an honor."

"I thank you for bringing me such a stunning lineup of young women," he said happily. "I cannot wait to see you girls wearing my designs." He waved his hand to some of the sketches on the walls. "This gives you a little sneak preview, but the designs have changed considerably since these were done. You will see that later. First, I want you to meet a friend of mine." He nodded to a pretty young woman who was sitting off to one side of the room. "This is Ramona Winters. She's an actor, currently starring in an Off-Broadway show." He winked at her. "Although the word on the street is that it may not be *Off* Broadway for long."

She smiled. "I hope you're right."

"Anyway, I invited Ramona here to help coach you girls in regard to attitude." He pointed to Grandmother. "As Katherine can attest, attitude in fashion is everything."

"That's right." Grandmother nodded.

"So, if you'll excuse me. I'll leave you to Ramona for an hour. Then you will join me in the fitting room … and the real fun will begin."

"Okay," Ramona said after Dylan left. "In one word, the look Dylan wants is fresh. But not smiley fresh. And we don't want the old model pout either. We're tired of that bored but irritated look. We want our models to have expressions that are pleasant without being overly happy. We want eyes that are clear, but not too bright. And we want a comfortable sort of confidence. Not arrogance, mind you. We don't want our models to look cocky, but we do want them to be assured. And you need to look like you're having fun, but not too much fun." She laughed. "Does that make any sense?"

There were a few questions, and for the next hour Ramona practiced expressions with the girls. Then before they ended, she called Taylor to the front of the room. "I want Taylor to strike some poses … since she really seems to grasp what we're going for here. Do you mind, Taylor?"

Taylor shrugged. "Not at all."

"See," said Ramona as Taylor did some poses. "Her features are relaxed yet pleasant. And she looks completely comfortable, but not haughty." Ramona glanced at Eliza now. "That

176

haughty expression might work for some designers, but it's not what Dylan is after." She clapped her hands. "We're out of time. It's on with the show and off to your fittings!"

"Who would've guessed that Taylor would be *teacher's pet*," Eliza said snidely as they headed out of the conference room.

"Is somebody jealous?" teased Casey.

"Hardly." Eliza flipped hair over her shoulder and laughed as she linked arms with Daisy. "I just think it's funny that Taylor has gone from bad girl to Little Miss Perfect. Amazing how a little time in rehab changes a person."

"Get over yourself," Casey hissed at her. Fortunately, Taylor said nothing. But DJ could see the fire in her eyes. She hoped Taylor wouldn't fall for Eliza's bait. The last thing Dylan needed for his big debut was a catfight!

17

NEW YORK DEBUT

FORTUNATELY, THE ONLY FUR THAT FLEW at Friday's first fitting was faux. Eliza actually minded her manners. DJ had noticed her grandmother taking Eliza aside. Apparently, she'd overheard Eliza slamming Taylor. After that, Eliza was fairly quiet and, although she was still in a snit, she wasn't taking it out on anyone. This was a relief, since it was clear that Taylor was getting the bulk of attention from Dylan—plus she was getting the best outfits, not to mention compliments.

"Now, if you'll just move to the city and model exclusively for me ..." he told Taylor as she did a turn so he could admire his workmanship.

"Maybe someday," she said with a coy expression.

"Just don't forget who helped you get your start in the fashion world," he teased.

Dylan also seemed to take a real shine to Daisy. "I think this one's got a future in fashion too," he told Grandmother as he made some final adjustments to the short plaid skirt she was trying on with a pair of tall boots. "Her legs just go on and on forever."

179

DJ was thankful to get through the fitting without making any serious blunders. Despite the way Haley and Ariel seemed to look up to her, DJ felt she was the least of the nine models. And she also felt she was the most likely to mess up the show. Well, other than the possibility that Eliza might attempt to wreak some kind of revenge against Taylor.

Later that evening, Grandmother treated the girls to a Broadway musical. She apologized that the only show she was able to get ten tickets for was *Grease*, but everyone thoroughly enjoyed it. Even Eliza, who had initially complained that it would be "lame," seemed to have liked it just fine. DJ had even caught her laughing and smiling a time or two.

On Saturday morning, Eliza was irked to discover that everyone except for her and Daisy had made plans to continue their Garment District tour.

"You guys can come along too," offered Rhiannon. "Just keep in mind it's a lot of walking."

"And knockoff shopping," added Casey. Then she turned to Kriti. "Sorry, I didn't mean that in a bad way."

"Reproductions, knockoffs, whatever you want to call them." Kriti smiled. "But keep in mind that what my father does is legal. He's careful not to copy anything that's licensed. My uncle is an attorney."

"Well, thanks but no thanks. Trekking around Manhattan in ugly shoes and shopping for counterfeits is not very enticing." Eliza turned to Daisy, who seemed to be thinking otherwise. "There are still a lot of shops we haven't seen yet."

Daisy nodded, but she looked a little disappointed. "See you guys later," she called as Eliza tugged her away.

"Poor Daisy," said Casey. "Maybe we should rescue her."

"Or do an intervention," said Kriti. They all laughed.

"Except that if we rescued Daisy, Eliza would have to come with us too," DJ pointed out.

"That's right," said Casey. "No one's allowed to be alone in the city. Although I'm pretty sure Miss Eliza Wilton can take care of herself."

"Pity the mugger that tries to steal her new Marc Jacobs bag from her," said DJ.

"She'd kick where it counts with her new Prada boots," added Casey.

"Oh, you guys!" Rhiannon shook her head. "Now, we've got a lot of ground to cover before our dress rehearsal. Let's get moving!"

And they did cover a lot of ground and, despite comfortable shoes, some of the girls were starting to complain.

"Last stop is my dad's company," Kriti told them. "And he's got a comfortable sales room where he entertains his buyers. You can put your feet up if you like."

"We'll call ahead for a taxi to take us back to Dylan's," offered DJ.

Kriti's dad was very gracious. He treated them like they were important buyers. He showed them his latest pieces and then allowed Kriti to take them through the factory. At the end, he gave them a discount on purchasing the reproduction bags of their choice—at his cost!

"Wow," said Ariel as they waited for the taxi. "I can't believe I have a real Versace bag."

"It's not real," DJ reminded her.

"But it looks real. I'll bet no one will know, and I'm not telling."

"Let's all make a pact," said Haley eagerly. "We won't tell anyone that these are knockoffs."

"Except my mother," said Ariel. "She'd wonder where I got five grand to lay down for a purse like this."

"It's useless to make a pact anyway," DJ said. "*Eliza* will know."

"And Eliza will tell," added Casey.

"Oh, yeah . . ." Ariel nodded. "What's up with her anyway? I used to think she was kind of nice, but she's been a real witch on this trip."

"Didn't you hear that Harry broke up with her?" asked Haley.

"Yeah, but why is she taking it out on us?"

"She's taking it out on Taylor," Casey corrected her.

"That's right," said Taylor. "She thinks I stole her man."

"Did you?" asked Ariel.

"No, I did not. But I'm starting to have second thoughts."

Then the taxi arrived. At first the driver started to complain about seven girls piling into his car.

"Don't worry," Taylor told him as she slid into the front seat next to him. "We tip well."

He laughed. "And you're not too hard on the eyes either."

Taylor told him where to take them. "And step on it," she said, "Please."

He did step on it, so much so that DJ, crammed in the center of the backseat, started to feel carsick. But they made it to the studio a couple of minutes before two. Taylor paid and tipped the driver. Then they went inside to discover that, once again, they'd beaten Eliza and Daisy. But Grandmother was there.

"Just on time." She sounded relieved as she looked over the girls. "But there are only seven of you. Where are the others? Daisy and Eliza?"

"We went our separate ways today," DJ explained. "They went shopping."

"Well, the limos are waiting," said Grandmother. "And Dylan and Ramona are all ready to head over to Bryant Park. We have the use of the catwalk only between three and five, although Dylan thought if we got there early we might be able to squeeze in some extra time. Why don't some of you ride with them?" She looked over the group. "Taylor, Desiree, Casey, Rhiannon, you four go with Dylan. We'll wait for Daisy and Eliza. Tell Dylan we'll be along presently."

The first limo arrived at Bryant Park, but the other one didn't seem to be following, and it was already 2:30. The cat-walk was free, so naturally, Dylan was pushing to "get the show on the road." DJ called her grandmother to check on the others.

"Those silly girls didn't make it back here," growled Grandmother. "I just called Eliza, and she's still waiting for a taxi in who knows where. I told her to go directly to Bryant Park—and if a taxi doesn't get there in five minutes, I told her to walk. Shoes or no shoes! The other girls and I are on our way to Bryant Park now, but traffic is horrible. Tell Dylan we'll catch up with him as soon as we can. In the meantime, you go ahead and get started."

DJ relayed this information, and Dylan and Ramona began putting the four girls through their paces, practicing on the catwalk, which wasn't all that different than the one Grandmother had gotten for them at home. But they were still wearing their street clothes when Grandmother and the other girls arrived.

"Still no sign of Daisy or Eliza?" Grandmother asked DJ. "I was hoping they'd beat us here."

"We haven't seen them." DJ forced a smile. "Don't worry, Grandmother, I'm sure they'll be here soon."

Grandmother shook her head in dismay. "I'm very surprised and disappointed in Eliza. I thought she had better manners than this."

DJ just shrugged. But it was her turn to do the walk again. *Think fresh, relaxed, confident, having fun, but not too much fun,* she kept telling herself as she walked. *Shoulders back, head up, legs moving in a straight line.* It was a lot to remember, but the more she did it, the easier it became.

"Lost?" DJ heard her grandmother shouting. "How can you possibly be lost? You're only a few blocks away from here. No, it's on *Sixth* Avenue. You need to go *east*, Eliza." She paused. "How should I possibly know whether it's right or left. Good grief!" Grandmother held her phone out to one of Dylan's design assistants. "Please, help this poor witless child find her way over here."

The assistant chuckled as she took the phone and attempted to explain directions.

"They're trying to talk Eliza and Daisy in," explained DJ as she rejoined the other girls. "And my grandmother sounds ticked."

They continued practicing their runs on the catwalk. Between the advice from Grandmother, Dylan, and Ramona, DJ suddenly felt like she got it. Like it was starting to make sense.

"That's beautiful," called out Dylan as DJ made her final walk back. "Spot on, Desiree!" DJ gave him a slight nod and then told herself to think of this simply as an athletic event. Just like in swimming, volleyball, basketball, or soccer, she knew how to tell her body to do certain things in certain ways, to practice them enough, and just like in sports training, she eventually was able to *just do it*.

"Okay, let's head for the dressing room now," called out Dylan's number-one design assistant, a short brunette named Camilla.

"What about the other girls?" complained Dylan. "Shouldn't we—"

"We can't keep waiting on them," said Camilla sharply. She looked at her watch. "We're already running late now. We're supposed to vacate by five, and the Maurice Bernard people are scheduled for six. We gotta keep it moving, Dylan."

And so they did keep it moving. It wasn't until the girls were into their second outfits that Eliza and Daisy finally showed up. Burdened down with shopping bags and complaining about their aching feet—no wonder since they both insisted on wearing their ridiculously uncomfortable designer shoes—the two girls both acted put out for their inconveniences.

"Get undressed," Camilla commanded.

"I can't believe we had to walk here!" Eliza tossed down her bags and kicked off her new red Manolo Blahnik shoes like they were trash—the same costly shoes she'd been bragging about at dinner last night.

"Well, I can't believe it took us an hour to go a few blocks!" exclaimed Daisy as she peeled off her skirt. "Those were looong blocks!"

"I can't believe you girls are *this* late," said Camilla as she and the other wardrobe assistants worked to get Daisy and Eliza dressed.

"It's not our fault this stupid town doesn't have enough taxis," snapped Eliza.

"You should have planned better," Camilla snapped back at her. "We're supposed to be out of here by five, and we'll need to move fast if we want to get through a complete dress rehearsal now. You girls are wearing your third outfits now. Everybody move fast!"

Although they moved as fast as they could, they were barely able to squeeze in one complete run through with three sets of wardrobe changes. By the time the lights and music went down, the Maurice Bernard people were already showing up—and complaining that Dylan's group was stealing their time.

"We're out of here," Camilla snarled back at one of their design assistants. "Models, you go ahead and wear those outfits back to the studio. We'll do our final adjustments and change there!" She shouted out orders to the rest of the crew, and poor Dylan hovered in a corner, looking like he was about to fall apart.

Grandmother went over to join him, consoling him and assuring him that all would be well by Monday's preview show with the photographers. Meanwhile, everyone scrambled to gather their things and load up the vans and get out of the way before too many in the Maurice Bernard group went ballistic. One Bernard model had already cleared off a bench by sweeping the girls' personal belongings into a heap on the floor.

"The fashion world waits for no one," joked Taylor as the girls fished through the pile of clothes, shoes, and bags to pick out their own things.

"It's only three minutes past five," DJ pointed out as they dashed out to the loading area. "I don't see why it's such a big deal."

"Three minutes may not seem like much," Grandmother breathlessly said after they were seated inside the limo, "but

I've seen designers nearly come to fisticuffs over such trivialities before. Fashion is serious business."

"I'm exhausted," admitted DJ as she leaned back in the seat. "Who knew that modeling was like an Olympic event?"

"Models must be strong," said Grandmother. Then she smiled. "You performed very well out there today, Desiree. As did you, Taylor. And all of you girls, for that matter." She smiled at Rhiannon and Casey too. "I was proud of my girls." She cleared her throat. "Rather, I was proud of most of them. Eliza has severely disappointed me."

"She'll get it together in time for the real show," said Rhiannon.

"Let's certainly hope so." Grandmother opened her bag and pulled out her cell phone. "Now I must cancel our dinner reservation."

"*Why?*" asked DJ. All afternoon, she'd been looking forward to eating at the fancy five-star restaurant Grandmother had raved about. It was Italian and supposedly one of Manhattan's best. Grandmother had made the reservation weeks ago.

"Because we'll never make it there in time."

"Thanks to Eliza," whispered Casey as Grandmother made her call.

"Don't make it any worse than it is," Rhiannon quietly warned as Grandmother politely apologized for the inconvenience.

Taylor nodded. "Mrs. Carter has enough on her plate."

"Looks like we'll be calling room service tonight," said Grandmother.

"Can't we find another restaurant?" asked DJ.

"Calling this late on a Saturday night?" Grandmother scowled. "And with a party of ten? Not any place I'd care to eat."

So it was that the girls ate in their rooms.

"What a pathetic way to spend Saturday night in New York," Eliza loudly complained from her room. It was well past nine by now, and DJ and Taylor were in their room along with Casey and Rhiannon. The nine girls had split into various rooms to watch different movies on pay-per-view. But the door adjoining the the other room was still open, and Eliza's grumblings were hard to ignore.

"And whose fault is that?" called out Casey in an aggravated tone.

"New York taxi drivers," said Eliza.

"Like Mrs. Carter keeps telling you," said Rhiannon, "you can't rely on taxis to get you anyplace on time."

"That's why one hires a limo," Eliza shot back.

DJ turned up the volume on the TV and wished the girls would quit yelling.

"And that's so easily done during Fashion Week." Taylor's tone was sarcastic as she picked up a fat copy of *InStyle* magazine and began flipping through.

"Thanks for that helpful little news flash," said Eliza in her snootiest voice.

"You are oh so very welcome, Miss Eliza, dear," called Taylor in a faux southern accent that sounded remarkably like Eliza's.

When Eliza stuck her head into their room, DJ paused the movie and prepared herself to intervene. This was starting to sound like a real catfight. But to her surprise, Eliza was smiling. Okay, it wasn't a sincere-looking smile. But it wasn't exactly hostile either.

"Who wants to go out with me tonight?" Eliza was using her saccharine sweet tone now.

"I'll go," called Daisy from the other room.

"Anyone else want to catch some of that great city night-life?" Eliza tried again. "Taylor, how about you?"

Taylor actually looked slightly interested, then just shook her head and refocused her attention on her magazine.

"Come on," urged Eliza. "It'll be fun. Gorgeous models out on the town. Remember Vegas?"

Taylor just flipped a page, and DJ turned the movie back on. "No one is interested in going out tonight," she informed Eliza. "Besides, Grandmother made it clear that we can't be out at night without her or Inez to—"

"Oh, that's right." Eliza suddenly turned snooty again. "I'll be sure to invite Inez to go out with us."

"Then don't make any plans to go out," DJ said firmly.

"Who died and made you Mrs. Carter?"

DJ didn't honor that with an answer. But after the movie ended and she saw that Eliza and Daisy were actually getting dressed for what appeared to be a night out, she decided to leave the door between the two rooms open. And finally, when it looked like Eliza and Daisy were actually going to venture out, DJ stepped in.

"Seriously, you guys," she looked directly at Eliza, "if you go out without an escort, I *will* tell my grandmother."

"So, you've turned into a tattletale?" Eliza frowned. "How lame is that?"

DJ just rolled her eyes. "Just be warned."

"Maybe we better not," said Daisy.

"Don't be a baby," Eliza told Daisy, then turned back to DJ. "For your information, Rat Girl, we're just going downstairs *to the lobby*. Any rules against that? Or are we under house—or should I say—room arrest?"

DJ frowned. Now she actually wasn't too sure. Grandmother hadn't said anything about what they did within the confines of the hotel. Still, she didn't trust Eliza not to venture farther. So DJ directed her next warning to Daisy. "You need to understand this, Daisy," she said in a serious tone, "my grandmother will pull you from the show if you do not abide by her rules." DJ put her face close to Daisy's now. "Do you fully get that?"

Daisy looked slightly nervous then nodded. "Yeah, sure."

"And you have really looked forward to this," DJ reminded her. "It would be sad if you blew it and missed out."

"And Mrs. Carter will probably make you pay her back," Casey called out as she got her shoes on, getting ready to head back to her own room. "You'll have to cover your expenses if you don't model."

"Don't worry about that nonsense," Eliza told Daisy. "Come on, the night is young."

DJ thought she might've put the fear of God — or maybe Grandmother — into Daisy. But whether that was enough to make Eliza behave remained to be seen. Casey and Rhiannon returned to their room, and Taylor continued reading her magazine, and it was close to ten when Kriti stuck her head in the doorway.

"Where did Eliza and Daisy go?" she asked.

"Who cares." Taylor flipped a page of her magazine and yawned.

DJ quickly explained.

Kriti frowned. "And Mrs. Carter is okay with that?"

Now DJ felt worried. Fair or not, she knew that Grandmother had specifically asked her to take responsibility for the girls in the two adjoining rooms. Would Grandmother blame her for Eliza's bad choices? DJ began pacing, trying to decide what to do.

"Are you going to tell Mrs. Carter?" asked Taylor without looking up from her magazine.

"You think I should?"

"Probably."

DJ nodded and went directly to her grandmother's room, knocked on the door, and tried not to look surprised when Grandmother answered in a hotel bathrobe with her face encased in a green facial masque. "What is it now?" she demanded.

"Sorry to disturb you." Then DJ quickly relayed that Eliza and Daisy were AWOL. "They might just be in the hotel lobby ... but I can't guarantee it."

The green masque over Grandmother's forehead crackled. "Oh, dear!"

"I just thought you should know ... since you told me to help keep an eye on things."

"Yes. I do appreciate that. *Those foolish girls!*" She shook her head and more of her masque cracked. "Would you mind, Desiree, going down to check on them ... to see if they're really in the lobby and not getting into any trouble?"

"Okay."

"And, don't go alone. Please, take someone with you. Perhaps Rhiannon. She's a sensible girl."

"Do you want me to call you?"

"Yes, of course."

So DJ went back to her room, but instead of Rhiannon, who had already returned to her room, DJ asked Taylor. "Do you mind?"

Taylor grinned. "No. It might be fun being on the other side of trouble for a change. Let me get my shoes on."

"And I'll tell Kriti what's up."

Soon, Taylor and DJ were down in the lobby. They searched everywhere and finally spied the two girls in the bar. And, already, they'd managed to connect with a couple of older-looking guys.

"What do we—"

"Come with me," said Taylor as she marched straight into the bar and up to the pub table where she tapped Eliza on the shoulder. Eliza turned in surprise, then smiled. "You decided to join us after—"

"Hey, gorgeous," the blond guy said to Taylor. "Can I buy you a drink?"

"No, thanks." Taylor looked evenly at him. "And you can't buy these girls drinks either. They are underage, and their chaperone will be down here any minute to get them."

Daisy jumped down from her chair and looked toward the door. "Let's go," she said quickly.

"Good thinking," said DJ as she linked arms with her.

"Come on," Taylor told Eliza. "Party's over."

Eliza and Daisy didn't say anything as they rode the elevator up, but DJ could tell they were nervous. It took all of her self-control not to chuckle at how coolly Taylor had handled the situation.

"You guys better get into your pajamas and look like you've been in your room for a while," DJ told them as they went to their separate rooms. "I'll tell Grandmother you're back. But she'll probably do a bed check tonight." Then she closed the adjoining room and burst into giggles.

Taylor grinned. "What's so hilarious?"

"You," admitted DJ. "You were awesome down there."

"Hey, I learned from the best."

"Huh?"

"You, silly! Remember all those times you rescued me in Vegas?"

DJ laughed. "I tried to forget."

"You better go tell your grandmother our lost girls are back."

So DJ returned to Grandmother's room to find that her face was no longer green and, instead of the bathrobe, she had on her pale pink silk pajamas and matching robe. DJ informed her that they'd found them. And, when she asked where, DJ was honest. Grandmother sadly shook her head. "I will be so relieved when Fashion Week is over."

"I'm sorry that Eliza is acting like this," DJ told her.

Now Grandmother actually put a hand on DJ's shoulder and smiled. "I so appreciate your help, Desiree. I know I haven't been the best grandmother to you, and we don't always see eye to eye on things. But I am very proud of you, and I am extremely grateful for the level of maturity you display."

"Thanks."

"Might I ask you one more favor, Desiree?"

"What is it?"

"Would you please do what you can to keep tabs on Eliza and Daisy during your day off tomorrow? I'm perfectly willing to send those two home if needed, but I know how Dylan has planned for all nine girls in his show. This is his big debut, Desiree. I hate to spoil it for him."

The last thing DJ wanted was to be stuck with Eliza all day, but she understood Grandmother's dilemma too. "Want to make a deal?" she asked.

"What's that?"

"If you'll start calling me DJ instead of Desiree, I will stick to Eliza like glue until the fashion show."

"Desiree is such a beautiful name. Why don't you like it?"

"I like it okay, Grandmother, I just don't feel like it fits me. Or maybe I have to grow into it. All my *real friends* call me DJ."

"*DJ.*" Grandmother's mouth twisted as if she'd just bitten into a lemon. "Well, I suppose I can get used to it, *DJ.*"

"Thanks!" DJ grinned. "Then it's a deal. Oh, yeah, I told Eliza and Daisy that you'd be doing a bed check tonight."

Grandmother's eyes lit up. "That's a splendid idea. In fact, I will do that every night until we go home, Desiree—excuse me, I meant, DJ."

Everyone slept in late on Sunday. Everyone except DJ. She knew she needed to get up early to do two things. The first thing was to spend some quiet time with God and to read her Bible. She knew she was going to need God's help more than ever now that she was supposed to run herd on Eliza. But the second reason she'd gotten up early was to think of a plan to lure Eliza into doing something besides shopping. All of the girls, except Eliza and Daisy, planned to go sight-seeing today—to act like corny tourists. But how could she talk Eliza into something like that? And so she prayed about it.

Then, to DJ's amazement, it all fell into place at breakfast. All the girls were so excited about having a whole day to see all the sites that suddenly, Daisy was interested too. That's where DJ stepped in. "Come with us, Daisy," she urged her. "It's going to be a blast."

"Yeah," agreed Casey. "We're going to do the double-decker bus and the Empire State building and everything."

"Okay," said Daisy eagerly.

"But what about—"

DJ cut Eliza off. "That means you'll have to come with us too, Eliza," she said quickly, glancing at Grandmother who appeared to be perusing a Fashion Week magazine, but DJ suspected she was listening. "Because the rules say, 'no girls alone in the city,' remember?"

Eliza scowled.

"That's right," said Grandmother, looking up. "No girls alone in the city, Eliza. Is that clear?"

"Yes, Mrs. Carter."

Grandmother smiled. "Good."

And it was good. To everyone's surprise, Eliza was fairly congenial, and she actually seemed to have a good time as they toured the highlights of the city. Oh, she let out an occasional grumble, like when Casey pretended to be King Kong on top of the Empire State Building. But for the most part, the day went smoothly. But DJ made sure to keep a safe distance between Eliza and Taylor.

On Sunday night, Grandmother had preordered breakfast for all the girls for the next morning—her way to ensure they were out of the hotel on time for their appointment with Dylan at ten. On Monday morning, the room-service carts were lined up in the hallway, and soon everyone was finished with breakfast. They all crowded into Grandmother's suite so she could give them their morning pep talk. "I expect nothing short of professionalism from each and every one of you today," she told them. "I have promised Dylan that you will all do your very best and no one will be disappointed." Then she quickly reiterated their schedule. "Dylan's studio at ten for the final fitting. Then, we'll head back to Bryant Park for the last dress rehearsal and the photo shoot and, if we're lucky, we'll have some media people there too. Everyone is interested in seeing a show with nine teen girls from the same town." Grandmother smiled. "I do hope you'll all do your very best, girls."

"I was mistaken as Paris Hilton in the lobby yesterday," Eliza informed them as they rode over to Dylan's studio.

"Seriously?" Casey frowned at her. "Did the person need glasses?"

"No, it happens all the time," said Eliza lightly. "Right, Daisy?"

Daisy nodded. "Oh, yeah."

"I hope Paris isn't too worried," said Grandmother dryly. DJ couldn't help but laugh.

The fitting went fairly smoothly, and the rehearsal and photo shoot at Bryant Park was relatively painless. But when the media people, who had actually showed up, focused most of their attention on Taylor (somehow the word slipped out that she was Eva Perez's daughter), Eliza got into a little snit.

"Go tell the press that I am Eliza Wilton," she whispered to Daisy, "heiress to the Wilton fortune."

Daisy reluctantly obeyed, but apparently that didn't impress them much. Although Daisy must've impressed them, because they kept her for a while, shooting photos and doing an impromptu interview. And next they went for DJ.

"You're Katherine Carter's granddaughter?" the woman began as cameras rolled, photos were snapped, and others listened. DJ acknowledged this, as well as about a dozen other questions about life in Crescent Cove, trying to convince the woman that she was just an ordinary girl. But it was obvious by her questions that the interviewer was skeptical.

"DJ's telling the truth," Taylor assured the woman and the other press who had gathered around. "DJ is about the most ordinary girl I know. She wears smelly tennis shoes sometimes, goes out for sports, won a write-in election as homecoming queen, and even got hit by a car when she saved the life of a little boy." Of course, that interested them. And Taylor was happy to fill them in on all the details. "Just look it up online; it was in all the local news," she finally told them.

"This is a good story," the interviewer told DJ as she handed her and Taylor business cards. "But I might need to call for some follow-up questions." She nodded over to Grandmother. "But I know how to reach you."

196

"Time to clear out of here," called Camilla.

They gathered their stuff and piled back into the limos. As DJ was about to slip the business card into her bag, Eliza snatched it. "That woman was from *Vogue*?"

DJ just shrugged.

"Of course," said Grandmother as she took the card from Eliza and slipped it into her own bag. "Why wouldn't she be?"

Eliza leaned back into the seat, folding her arms across her front with narrowed eyes and making a noise that sounded a lot like "harrumph."

"Tomorrow is the big day," Grandmother said as they all sat around a long table in the hotel restaurant later that night. "Dylan's big debut." She smiled. "And yours too." It was only a one-day show—one chance for a designer to shine. The girls knew how important it would be to Dylan Marceau's career. Even Eliza seemed to be taking it more seriously now. Oh, she might be having periodic fits of jealousy, but at least she seemed to be cooperating. Still, DJ knew that she had to hang tight with Eliza for tomorrow morning. She had to make sure that Eliza stayed out of trouble and arrived in time for the show. For this, DJ thought she should get combat pay.

On Tuesday, Eliza, Taylor, Daisy, and DJ went to a matinee that ended with plenty of time to make it to Dylan's studio for hair and makeup and finally the ride over to Bryant Park.

As they were getting into their first outfits, DJ was suddenly a bundle of nerves. She actually felt slightly lightheaded and afraid that she might faint. She went over to a chair on the sidelines and sat down.

She bent over and took a deep breath, then felt a hand on her shoulder. To her surprise it was Eliza. "Butterflies?" she asked her.

DJ nodded.

"Just breathe slowly," said Eliza. "And think about something you love to do." She laughed. "Like basketball."

DJ took a slow breath and stood. "Thanks."

"Let me help you with that," said Eliza as she reached over to straighten the collar of the tweed jacket that DJ was wearing. "You look great, by the way."

DJ frowned. "Why are you being nice to me?"

Eliza shrugged. "I could ask you the same thing."

"Huh?"

"You've been nice to me."

"I have?"

Eliza laughed. "Well, I could be wrong. But it seems like you have. I mean, you've been including me in things. You kept your grandmother from sending me home."

"I did?"

"That's what Mrs. Carter told me."

DJ smiled, but wasn't sure what to say. "Well, this show means a lot to her ... and Dylan too. It seems like we should give it our best."

And that's what they did. Oh, there were a few little missteps to start with. Casey came out too soon on the first run and nearly knocked Kriti over. Then Ariel tripped over a piece of carpet that had come untacked, but at least she didn't fall. Still, the audience, which actually had some celebrities in it, didn't seem to mind. As the show progressed, they became very energetic and enthused.

"Hold still," one of the assistants told DJ back in the dressing room. "I need to fix that hem before you go out."

DJ had just slipped into her second outfit, a formal holiday dress out of a dark blue taffeta that reminded DJ of an oil slick. Okay, she knew that wasn't how Dylan would describe it, but the colors in the fabric seemed to change depending on the angle and light.

"I'm sorry," DJ said as she waited for the girl to repair what had come undone. She was using some kind of special tape. "Did I do that?"

"It happens." The girl used her fingers to press it back into place, then stood and nodded. "That should hold it."

"It's really a beautiful dress," DJ said as she did a little spin to see how the full skirt flared out.

"Get into these shoes," commanded another assistant, pulling them out of the numbered box.

DJ shoved her feet into the velvet shoes, waiting as the woman tied the bows, adjusting them to perfection. Meanwhile, one of the guys put a necklace that looked expensive around her neck. And then earrings and a bracelet too. DJ waited, standing perfectly still. Maybe this was how it felt to be a princess. And, okay, it was kind of interesting, but not something DJ would want to do on a regular basis. She grinned at Taylor, suppressing the urge to yell, "break a leg," as Taylor got ready to take her turn on the runway. Once again, Taylor looked stunning. She had on espresso-brown pants that fit perfectly, a faux fur jacket that looked like a million bucks, and a killer pair of boots. But even without the outfit, Taylor would've looked stunning. It was just who she was. It was no wonder that she'd become Dylan's favorite. The director cued Taylor to go. Kriti was next, which meant DJ needed to be ready to follow her.

"You're doing great," DJ bent down so Kriti could hear her.

"Thanks." Kriti looked nervous. "I just hope I don't trip or get knocked down this time."

"Dylan seems very pleased with you," DJ reminded her. "I heard him mentioning that he'd like to use you for a print ad."

Kriti smiled happily. "Can you believe it?"

"Sure."

Now the director nudged Kriti, and she stood straight and headed out for her turn on the catwalk. DJ listened to the crowd respond. And, not for the first time, DJ thought that Dylan had been smart to include "normal-looking" girls in his big debut. Sure, they weren't all "normal-looking," but there seemed to be a nice balance of normal against the ones like Taylor, Eliza, and even Daisy.

DJ felt surprisingly good as she took her turn now, strutting down the high and narrow catwalk, feeling like a rock star as the music blared and the lights flashed. Once again, she imagined she was participating in an athletic event, giving it her all, focusing on each step and each turn, playing her best game.

It seemed that all the girls were on top of it tonight. By the time the show ended, it seemed that Dylan Marceau and the Carter House girls (as the press insisted on calling them) were quite a hit in their New York debut.

In fact, when it was over the audience gave the girls and Dylan a standing ovation. Grandmother said that was something that didn't happen a lot—especially not for a first-time showing.

Later that night, they celebrated their successful show at the five-star Italian restaurant Grandmother had been raving about. One of her friends had somehow gotten a reservation for ten. The food was fabulous, but DJ was almost too tired to enjoy it. The other girls were a mix of excitement and exhaustion, and everyone seemed satisfied that they'd done their best. DJ was just thankful that no catfights had erupted.

"Guess what?" Taylor said later that night, as they were getting ready for bed.

"What?" asked DJ sleepily.

200

"An agency called."

"An agency?" DJ tried to figure out what that meant.

"A modeling agency."

"Oh?" DJ peered curiously at Taylor. "They called you?"

"Yeah ... offering a contract."

"To model? Professionally?"

Taylor chuckled. "Yeah, *professionally*. I guess that means I'll get paid."

"But you're only seventeen."

"That doesn't matter. There are models younger than that."

"Are you going to do it?"

Taylor shrugged. "I don't know."

"It's what you've wanted, isn't it?"

"Sort of."

"Did you tell my grandmother yet?"

"No." Taylor shook her head. "And don't tell her, okay?"

"Sure. Of course not."

"Because I'm not sure. And it's a pretty big agency ... I'm certain she'd think I should go for it."

DJ wanted to ask Taylor why she was unsure about this after having wanted it for so long, but she didn't know how to say it.

"I can tell by your face that you're puzzled." Taylor rubbed lotion onto her hands, forearms, and elbows—the same way she did every night before bed. "Go ahead, DJ, you can ask me why I'm not sure."

"Okay." DJ held up her hands. "Why?"

"Well, it's partially because I'm worried ... I mean, I'm barely out of rehab. What if I mess up ... what if I start drinking again?"

DJ nodded. "Yeah ... I wondered about that."

"But that's not the only reason."

"What?"

"Well, I didn't want to tell anyone ..." Taylor sat down on her bed and placed her hands in her lap.

"What?"

"If I tell you, you have to keep it a secret."

"You know you can trust me, Taylor." But even as she said this, DJ felt worried. What if it was something really huge? What if Taylor was in some serious kind of trouble?

"While I was in rehab ... I committed my life to God."

DJ blinked. "You did?"

Taylor nodded.

"But that's awesome, Taylor!" Despite being tired, DJ felt like dancing now. "That is so cool! Very, very cool. I'm so happy for you!"

Taylor smiled in a self-conscious way. "Thanks."

"But why do you want to keep that a secret?"

"Because I still make mistakes. I blow it. I shoot off my mouth, and I don't always act like a good Christian."

"And?" DJ thought Taylor could've been describing her.

"And I can't bear to have people thinking I'm a hypocrite."

DJ kind of laughed.

"Thanks." Taylor shook her head. "See what I mean."

"No, that's not it. Christians make mistakes, Taylor. I blow it all the time. Doing something wrong doesn't mean you're not a good Christian. In fact, I don't even know what a *good* Christian is, well, except maybe Rhiannon. But to be fair, she's always been a really sweet person. It's in her nature to be nice. Although she does take being a Christian seriously too. Still, next to her, I look like a mess a lot of the time. But I know that all I have to do is ask, and God forgives me. We have to forgive each other too. Maybe in time ... well, maybe we'll grow up some and we'll look and act like better Christians."

"Maybe."

"So, you really shouldn't keep it a secret. I mean, it's up to you, but I do think you should let others know. Rhiannon would be so stoked to hear about it. She and I have both been praying for you a lot."

"Thanks." Taylor stood back up. "But here's my next question ... I'm just not sure that being a Christian and being a professional model can really work. You know what I mean? We hear such sad stories about girls in this industry. What if I signed to model and fell off the wagon and lost my faith and totally messed up? Where would I be?"

"Back where you were at Christmastime?"

She nodded. "Exactly."

"But I'm not saying that's going to happen," DJ said quickly.

"But it might."

"So ... what are you going to do then?"

"I guess I'll do what my counselor back in rehab told me to do."

"What's that?"

"Take life one day at a time and pray about everything."

"Sounds like good advice to me." DJ sighed happily.

"And now I'm going to bed."

"Me too." DJ turned off the light.

"Good night, DJ."

"Good night, Taylor." DJ giggled. "Hey, we're related now, Taylor. We're both God's children—that makes us sisters."

"Good night, sis."

BIKINI BREAKDOWN

carter house girls

MELODY CARLSON

bestselling author

Read chapter 1 of *Bikini Breakdown*, Book 7 in Carter House Girls.

"I'm sorry, Mother, but I refuse to spend *my* spring break in some disgusting, dirty third world country." Eliza rolled her eyes dramatically for the benefit of her captive audience at the Carter House breakfast table. "That's just peachy that you and Dad don't mind being inoculated with all those toxic shots just so that you can use filthy outhouses, be devoured by mosquitoes, and sleep in rodent infested tents, but count me out."

Casey giggled and DJ glanced around to see if Grandmother was anywhere nearby. DJ knew she didn't like for the girls to use their cell phones at the table. But she also knew exceptions were sometimes made when it was a parent—especially when it was a parent of wealth or influence, like the Wiltons.

Eliza's forehead creased as she listened to whatever was being said on the other end of the phone. "Thanks anyway, Mother, but I'm passing. Honestly, I'd rather stay right here in boring old Crescent Cove than go with you guys to the ends of the planet. *Ya'll have fun now.*" Then she snapped her cell phone shut and used a foul word.

"Eliza Wilton," exclaimed Grandmother as she entered the dining room. "That's no way for a well-bred Kentucky debutante to speak."

"I'm sorry, Mrs. Carter." Eliza looked slightly embarrassed. "I'm just so frustrated with my mother!"

"Well, please do control yourself." Grandmother frowned as she sat down at her regular place at the head of the table and put her napkin in her lap. "Good morning, ladies."

Like well-trained robots, or Stepford teens, they all chirped back "good morning." And then Rhiannon asked the blessing. This was a relatively new development, but something that Rhiannon had volunteered to do. When both DJ and Taylor had backed her, Grandmother had agreed and later on even acted as if it had been her own idea in the first place.

After Rhiannon said "amen," she turned to Eliza. "So ... where does your mom want you to go for spring break anyway?"

"*Nepal.*" Eliza said the name of the country as if she was swearing again.

"I've heard Nepal is an interesting place." DJ refilled her coffee cup. "I'd love to go there someday."

Eliza made a face. "Great, I'll ask my parents if you can take my place."

"The mountains are beautiful there," Kriti said quietly.

"If I wanted to see mountains, I'd go to Switzerland," Eliza retorted.

"I think a trip to Nepal sounds like an adventure." Casey stabbed her fork into a piece of pineapple. "I'd be happy to go too."

"Maybe you and DJ should flip a coin." Eliza broke her toast in half. "To see which one of you can go."

"Well, DJ would need a passport," said Grandmother wryly. "And with only two weeks before spring break, I don't think it's very likely."

"Too bad." Eliza directed her sarcasm to DJ. "It would've been fun to see you coming home covered in mosquito bites and suffering from some rare form of tropical dysentery and—"

"*Eliza?*" Grandmother's brows arched in warning. Obviously her Botox was wearing off again.

"Sorry, Mrs. Carter." She made a sheepish smile. "I was just joking."

"Well then ..." said Grandmother. "As it turns out, I've already made plans for DJ and myself anyway."

DJ stopped with her spoonful of yogurt in midair. "Plans?"

"Yes. The general has graciously given me the use of his Palm Beach home during the week of spring break."

"Palm Beach, Florida?" asked Eliza with interest.

"Yes, of course."

DJ wasn't sure whether to be pleased or irritated. On one hand Palm Beach might be somewhat pleasant—sunshine and sand. But on the other hand, why hadn't Grandmother asked her *before* accepting the invitation for both of them?

Grandmother smiled at DJ. "Doesn't that sound lovely, dear?"

"I guess so."

"You *guess* so?"

"To be honest, you kind of took me by surprise, Grandmother."

"But isn't it a pleasant surprise?" Grandmother looked so hopeful that DJ forced herself to just smile and nod.

"Palm Beach sounds good to me." Taylor glanced out the window and saw it was raining again. "And I'm sure you won't miss this weather."

"My thinking precisely." Grandmother rubbed her wrist. "My arthritis has been acting up lately and I thought some warmth and sunshine would be most helpful."

"So . . ." Eliza began slowly, directing her comments to DJ's grandmother. "If you and DJ are in Palm Beach, does that mean Carter House will be vacated by everyone else that week?"

"Yes, of course." Grandmother put a spoonful of sugar substitute into her coffee and stirred. "I couldn't have you girls left here unsupervised."

"No, no . . . of course not." Eliza looked slightly miffed now, like maybe she'd planned on spending spring break in "boring old Crescent Cove." Actually, DJ wouldn't be surprised, since Eliza had recently developed a crush on a new guy at school. She probably hoped that she and Lane Harris would be dating by spring break. Perhaps she even imagined inviting him over to Carter House while everyone else was gone—and maybe they'd throw some huge house party and get into all kinds of trouble. That wouldn't surprise DJ a bit. It seemed that Eliza was steadily spinning out of control—like she thought someone was giving prizes for teenage girls with the most messed-up lives.

"So perhaps you'd like to rethink your decision about vacationing with your parents now." Grandmother peered curiously at Eliza.

"No, thank you." Eliza firmly shook her head. "I'd rather just go home to Louisville."

"And stay there by yourself?" Grandmother looked concerned.

"The household staff would be there."

Grandmother nodded sympathetically. "Yes, I suppose so." Now she smiled as if an idea was occurring to her. "You know, Eliza, the general's Palm Beach house is quite roomy. Perhaps you'd like to join us for—"

"*Grandmother!*" DJ felt alarmed now. The last thing she wanted was to be stuck down in Florida with Eliza Wilton for a whole week. And, besides, didn't Grandmother know how many things could go wrong during spring break—especially with someone like Eliza along?

"What is it, dear?"

"Don't you think you should consult me first?" DJ asked. "I thought it was just you and me going to Palm Beach and now you're inviting Eliza too." The dining room got very quiet and DJ could feel all eyes on her. "I mean, what if I decided to invite someone else to come without asking you first? How would you feel about that?"

"Well … I suppose that would be acceptable—it's a very large house, after all."

DJ looked hopefully at her other friends now. "Like what if Taylor or Casey or Rhiannon wanted to come." Then feeling bad, she quickly added, "And Kriti too—what if they all wanted to come down to Palm Beach. Shouldn't they be included too?"

"Are you saying you want to invite *all* the Carter House girls to come with us to Palm Beach?" Grandmother looked slightly appalled and not exactly pleased. DJ thought she had her grandmother in an awkward position with this idea. Surely, she'd reconsider her invitation to Eliza now.

"Why not?" said DJ. "It seems only fair. I mean, we shouldn't exclude anyone, should we? That doesn't seem very *polite*, does it, Grandmother?"

"Well ... no, I suppose it's not." Grandmother smiled stiffly and looked around the table. "All right then—let's make this official. I'd like to extend an invitation to any of you who'd like to join us in Palm Beach for spring break."

"Really?" Casey looked hopeful.

"Yes. Why not?" Grandmother's expression got serious now. "Of course, you'll need to obtain your parents' permission first. And I'll expect you to cover your own travel expenses. And to contribute to the cost of food and entertainment while we're down there. But, DJ is right; it's only fair to invite everyone along."

"I think that sounds awesome," said Casey. "I just hope my parents will let me go."

"You could tell them that airfare to Florida will probably be cheaper than to California," DJ told her.

"Good point."

"Count me in too," said Taylor. "My mom's touring the Midwest all month and I'm definitely not into seeing the great-American bread belt."

"I don't know if I'll be able to go." Kriti looked uncertain, like she wasn't sure that she was really wanted.

"Wouldn't Palm Beach be more fun than being stuck in the city?" DJ asked her. "I'd think your parents would be glad for you to have some fun, Kriti."

"That's right," added Casey. "You've been working so hard on keeping your grades up. You need a break."

"If it would help, maybe Grandmother can talk to your parents for you," suggested DJ.

"Of course, I'm happy to speak to them." Grandmother nodded as if this new plan was becoming more appealing. "And to anyone else's parents, for that matter."

It suddenly seemed that everyone was talking at once, excitedly planning for bikini shopping and flight booking and parental coaxing, before Grandmother interrupted to remind them that it was time to leave for school.

Then the girls hurried to gather their bags and coats, rushing outside and trying to avoid the rain as they rushed the two cars. This morning Rhiannon and Kriti were riding with Eliza in her little white Porsche. The others went with DJ. But as DJ started her car, it occurred to her that Rhiannon had been unusually quiet at breakfast. In fact, she'd never said a word, one way or the other, about joining them in Palm Beach.

DJ turned to Taylor, who was sitting in the passenger seat. "Do you think something's wrong with Rhiannon?"

"She did seem pretty quiet," said Taylor.

"I wonder if she's worried about money." Even as she said this, DJ felt pretty sure that was the problem. "She might not be able to afford Palm Beach for spring break."

"Duh." This came from Casey in the backseat.

DJ turned around as she backed out of the driveway and looked at Casey. "Okay, I know that's probably got something to do with it. But maybe that's not all. Because, now that I think about it, Rhiannon was quiet last night too. Is she okay?"

"I'm not supposed to say anything." Casey imitated zipping her lips.

"It's not something about Bradford, is it?" DJ glanced at Taylor. "I mean, he seems totally devoted to her."

"No, it's not Bradford," Casey retorted in a slightly know-it-all tone.

"Is it her mom?" asked Taylor.

Now Casey didn't say a thing.

"It is, isn't it?" persisted Taylor.

Still Casey remained silent.

DJ snickered as she drove toward school. "You're a great one for keeping a secret, Casey. You've pretty much divulged it has to do with Rhiannon's mom. Why not just tell us what's up? At least that way we can be praying for her."

"We know her mom's out of rehab," continued Taylor. "But has she fallen off the wagon already?"

"Don't say you heard it from me."

"So that's it?" asked DJ. "Her mom's using again?"

"That's what Rhiannon thinks. She hasn't heard from her mom for more than a week now. And they had been in contact almost every day before that."

"Well, my rehab counselor said that it's pretty common for a person in recovery to go back to their drug of choice ... at least once." Taylor sighed. "It kind of seals the deal."

"Huh?" DJ was confused.

"It's like a last painful reminder that you don't want to go back to your old ways." Taylor tipped down the visor and touched up her lip gloss in the mirror.

"But you haven't had a drink yet, have you, Taylor?" Casey asked.

"No way." Taylor firmly shook her head as she tossed the lip gloss back into her bag. "But that's probably because I'm actually scared to go back to that place. I'm afraid that if I drink again, even if it's just once ... well, that it'll be all over with and that I'll never get sober again."

"I suppose that's a healthy fear," admitted DJ. "But you're a strong person, Taylor. I'll bet you'd get it back together ... even if you did slip up."

"Maybe … But I just don't want to go there." Taylor was counting something on her fingers now. "Do you realize that I'm almost up to seventy-five days of sobriety now?"

"Congratulations!" DJ smiled at her. "We should throw you a party."

"No, thanks. I'll pass."

"Back to Rhiannon," said Casey. "What should we do?"

"I don't know what we *can* do." DJ pulled into the school parking lot, snagging a spot not too far from the main entrance. "Well, besides praying and being understanding."

"I know something we can do," said Taylor as they got out of the car. "We can all help get some money together for Rhiannon to go to Palm Beach with us. That might help distract her from her mom's messes."

"Yeah, she could focus on our messes instead," teased Casey.

"Actually, that's a great idea," said DJ as they hurried across the street. "I'm willing to contribute whatever I can for her."

"I wish I could help too," said Casey. "But I'll be doing well if I can get my parents to agree to pay my way."

Just then Taylor pointed to where Eliza and the others were going into the building ahead of them. "Maybe we can get Ms. Eliza Wilton to pitch in for Rhiannon. We all know she can afford it."

"We *know* she can afford it," said DJ. "But the big question is will she willingly fork it over?"

Taylor chuckled like she knew a secret. "Oh, I think we might be able to come up with some ways to influence her."

"But what if Rhiannon won't accept charity?" asked Casey as they jogged up the steps to the door. "She can be pretty sensitive about that kind of thing."

"Somehow we'll figure it out," DJ assured them. "Somehow *all* of the Carter House girls are going to make it to Palm Beach for spring break." Of course, even as she said this, she had some serious doubts. Was it really a good idea for all of them to be down in Florida together? What if things got out of hand? Even worse, what if Taylor fell off the wagon? Suddenly DJ envisioned the Carter House girls starring in a bad episode of *Girls Gone Wild*, with her grandmother having a major meltdown and everything just falling totally apart. But then she realized how ridiculous that image was and she couldn't help but laugh.

"What's so funny?" Casey shook the rain off of her jacket.

"I was just imagining spring break turning into spring breakdown." DJ chuckled.

"And what would be surprising about that?" asked Taylor.

As DJ hurried to first class, she had to wonder ... what *would* be so surprising about that?

Carter House Girls Series
from Melody Carlson

Mix six teenage girls and one '60s fashion icon (retired, of course) in an old Victorian-era boarding home. Add boys and dating, a little high school angst, and throw in a Kate Spade bag or two ... and you've got the Carter House Girls, Melody Carlson's new chick lit series for young adults!

Mixed Bags
Book One

Softcover • ISBN: 978-0-310-71488-0

Stealing Bradford
Book Two

Softcover • ISBN: 978-0-310-71489-7

Homecoming Queen
Book Three

Softcover • ISBN: 978-0-310-71490-3

Viva Vermont!
Book Four

Softcover • ISBN: 978-0-310-71491-0

Lost in Las Vegas
Book Five

Softcover • ISBN: 978-0-310-71492-7

New York Debut
Book Six

Softcover • ISBN: 978-0-310-71493-4

Books 7–8 coming soon!

A Sweet Seasons Novel
from Debbie Viguié!

They're fun! They're quirky! They're Sweet Seasons—unlike any other books you've ever read. You could call them alternative, God-honoring chick lit. Join Candy Thompson on a sweet, lighthearted, and honest romp through the friendships, romances, family, school, faith, and values that make a girl's life as full as it can be.

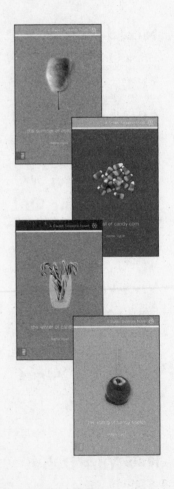

The Summer of Cotton Candy
Book One

Softcover • ISBN: 978-0-310-71558-0

The Fall of Candy Corn
Book Two

Softcover • ISBN: 978-0-310-71559-7

The Winter of Candy Canes
Book Three

Softcover • ISBN: 978-0-310-71752-2

The Spring of Candy Apples
Book Four

Softcover • ISBN: 978-0-310-71753-9

Pick up a copy today at your favorite bookstore!

Visit www.zondervan.com/teen

ZONDERVAN®
.com

Forbidden Doors

A Four-Volume Series from Bestselling Author Bill Myers!

Some doors are better left unopened.

Join teenager Rebecca "Becka" Williams, her brother Scott, and her friend Ryan Riordan as they head for mind-bending clashes between the forces of darkness and the kingdom of God.

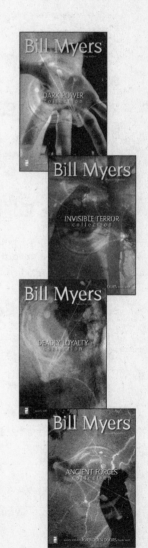

Dark Power Collection
Volume One

Softcover • ISBN: 978-0-310-71534-4

Contains books 1–3: *The Society*, *The Deceived*, and *The Spell*

Invisible Terror Collection
Volume Two

Softcover • ISBN: 978-0-310-71535-1

Contains books 4–6: *The Haunting*, *The Guardian*, and *The Encounter*

Deadly Loyalty Collection
Volume Three

Softcover • ISBN: 978-0-310-71536-8

Contains books 7–9: *The Curse*, *The Undead*, and *The Scream*

Ancient Forces Collection
Volume Four

Softcover • ISBN: 978-0-310-71537-5

Contains books 10–12: *The Ancients*, *The Wiccan*, and *The Cards*

Share Your Thoughts

With the Author: Your comments will be forwarded to the author when you send them to *zauthor@zondervan.com*.

With Zondervan: Submit your review of this book by writing to *zreview@zondervan.com*.

Free Online Resources at

www.zondervan.com

Zondervan AuthorTracker: Be notified whenever your favorite authors publish new books, go on tour, or post an update about what's happening in their lives.

Daily Bible Verses and Devotions: Enrich your life with daily Bible verses or devotions that help you start every morning focused on God.

Free Email Publications: Sign up for newsletters on fiction, Christian living, church ministry, parenting, and more.

Zondervan Bible Search: Find and compare Bible passages in a variety of translations at www.zondervanbiblesearch.com.

Other Benefits: Register yourself to receive online benefits like coupons and special offers, or to participate in research.